The Last Serial Killer

By

Rhonnie Fordham

Contents

Chapter 1

The summer of 1970 was hot, steamy, and sweaty. All the uncomfortable adjectives applied to Florida that year. Sure, early September was close to the freedom of fall, but damn sure not September fifth. Not two days away from Labor Day, and not during the notorious dog days.

Perry, Florida suffered a scorching summer. There was no wind, no relief. No release for the inconsequential inhabitants. Aside from the occasional trips to Tallahassee or Panama City Beach, the Perry people didn't have a whole lot out here. They had gas stations and catfish restaurants, but nothing else.

And this family at Everett's Mobile Home Parks had even less.

The white fence surrounding the entire lot was only a middle-class mirage. Trees were few and far between, and what little there were sparse with life. The same could be said for grass. Outside of small clusters at each trailer's front "yard," dirt was the sidewalk bonding this poor man's iteration of suburbia.

Everett's didn't exist for the view. Nor for the shotgun layout... The eight shabby single-wides somehow (and sadly) staying populated.

Like a lost commune, the renters didn't exist in Perry. Not to the townsfolk, at least. Or to the rest of Florida, for that matter.

Rarely did the Everett citizens ever travel beyond the cozy, impoverished confines of their beloved trailer park. There was a comfort when you shared a rural cage, after all. Shared despair. Misery loved company, and the people at Everett's were dumb but not delusional enough to know they couldn't go anywhere better or that such was even possible.

These were the usual suspects: senior citizens living off social security, drug addicts and drunks living off welfare and odd jobs, "rehabilitated" perverts forced outside the city limits, and families simultaneously broken and broke. Rarely were there any vacancies here at Everett's. Not with the low price and seclusion. Or the generations of losers trapped within this trailer park.

Hundreds of cars drove down Highway 60 every day, right past Everett's. All the cars in much better condition than the few pickups and Fords littering this lot's bumpy, barren attempts at driveways. But rarely did anyone stop by for a visit. Not until that stifling summer day. The day the stranger showed up.

He didn't quite fit the scene. Mark Mars said he saw the man emerge from the forest across the street. The closest to an origin story anyone had on the guy...

Being the resident elder of Everett's at the ripe age of seventy-seven, Mark didn't believe what he saw at first. He figured his sixth Dixie of the day had finally caught up to him.

So he stumbled out for a closer view on his rickety front porch. The afternoon sun forcing sweat into his baggy shirt and jean shorts.

And the more Mark watched, the more the stranger became all the more clearer. All the more closer.

The young man—or at least young to Mark's eyes—strolled across Highway 60. There were no cars in this heat. Not at one o'clock on an idyll Saturday when most of the community were long gone for Labor Day weekend. The stranger now had Everett's all to himself…not that Perry, Florida would ever care.

He was dressed nice enough for a club or a bar far from this trailer park. His muscular frame flashing in the tight velour short sleeve shirt and even tighter red flared pants. A headband wrapped around his flowing curly blonde hair. The large glasses an accessory to this All-American handsome face.

But still...something about the man seemed off to Mark. The stranger's slight smile sent Mark hiding behind the barrier of a battered screen door. Weak armor for sure, but a perfect spot for spectating. Even without air conditioning, Mark at least had that cold Dixie in his hand…

He watched the man pass the Everett's fence opening before coming to a stop right there at the start. At the beginning of the dirt road connecting these pathetic homes. At Everett's ecosystem.

There the stranger's smile disappeared as he scoped the remote terrain. A clear and perfect view of such a hideous and dismal "neighborhood." Only one family was on the outside. No gates were blocking this man. No trees could hinder his focus. No one could stop him.

What the hell's he looking for? Mark wondered.

Once the stranger's sights veered toward the screen door, Mark crouched down real quick, his knees cracking from an elderly boozer's rust. Breathing heavy, he didn't say a word. Didn't even take a sip of that Dixie. His heart pounded, the fear rising.

Something's not right with him…

To Mark's relief, the stranger looked off elsewhere. To another one of those identical eyesores.

The speed and the attention to detail startled Mark. Sent chills down his spine…especially how the man's blank glaze morphed into a glare.

He's like a fucking animal! Mark's drunk delirium worried. *Like a wolf on the prowl...*

In split seconds, the stranger marched toward his destination. The steps fast and frenetic, kicking up dust everywhere.

But what further terrified Mark was the sunlight glistening off the back of the man's waist. Off that Ruger Security-Six revolver tucked into his waistband for one shocking and scary "Mexican carry." The weapon polished and new and deadly.

Mark's panic accelerated once he saw where the stranger was going. Straight to the second trailer on the left. To the only people outside today on this scorching wasteland. This Southern-fried desert.

No! Why them?

*

A shirtless father was sitting by the cheap wading pool, his feet in the water as his overweight daughters ran wild in the bland blue contraption. The two girls in a child's euphoria. Both of them well under ten years old and clueless about their piss-poor poverty. Clueless to their family's suppressed status. Not that it mattered now. Not in this blissful moment.

Nearby, their mother oversaw burgers on the crooked grill. The cheapest brand possible for both grill and meat.

Together, the family formed a blue-collar paradise. The only American Dream attainable at such a trailer park. And one about to be ambushed.

The stranger got closer. No one was around to warn the family. Their momentary happiness enough to keep them oblivious. This level of joy too few and far between for Ben Slaughter's family to notice the armed animal on the attack.

*

Ben didn't have time to react. He was sixty-five and only in slightly better shape than Mark. Instead, he kept the focus on his girls Tina and Christine. Tina was eight and a year older than Christine. Their youth obvious in the face if not in their tall, rotund builds. The only difference being Christine's long dark hair to

Tina's sloppy bob cut. Their Southern accents matched by their parents. Not that Ben or his twenty-three-year-old wife Patsey were much different in physique. The couple's beer bellies bordered on obesity. Patsey's bikini unflattering everywhere except her height. After years of hard living, abuse, and poverty, Patsey's appearance somehow didn't look out of place next to a husband forty-nine years her senior. Even when Ben's gray beard looked to be made of Spanish moss.

Clinging to a Budweiser, a laughing Ben splashed water over his daughters. Their giggling much-needed music on this Everett's summer day.

The cultural contrast was evident the second the stranger stepped onto the scene. In front of the pool.

"Ben!" a worried Patsey yelled.

Startled, Ben looked right at the handsome man. The unease sinking in even as Christine and Tina's heavy weight sunk through the pool. He sat completely still on the lawnchair, the sunlight stinging his vision. But he could see enough. Enough to notice the man staring him down. *Glowering* at him.

"I got you!" Christine laughed.

The two girls kept playing tag in this white trash swimming pool. The space too small for their larger bodies.

Water splashed all across Ben, but he didn't flinch. He didn't even turn away from the quiet stranger.

Now Patsey took a few steps toward them, the greasy spatula still in her hand, the pathetic weapon. "Who are you?" she asked in a trembling tone.

Like an indifferent scientist, the man confronted her. His test subject. The Perry, Florida sun a spotlight to the pale skin and 70s fashion. "Are you Patsey Slaughter?" he asked in a stilted, dry voice.

Patsey just looked at him. All nervous and jittery.

All the while, Tina and Christine kept playing, cackling. Their noises the only ones in the silence. They splashed through the water with reckless abandon. A dumb naivety prevalent. Their interest only in the game, not the mystery.

The stranger waited in the tension. For an answer he already knew the answer to.

Just remember what they did, the stranger reminded himself. *Who they really are.*

"Uh, yes," Patsey finally said. She turned to Ben. "Do you know who—"

"Who the hell are you?" Ben barked to the man. He staggered to his feet, struggling to play tough when moving this sloppy and aching from painful joints and limbs he rarely used.

Not saying a word, the stranger faced him.

Ben waved the Budweiser at him. Now that Everett's side was taking over...all Southern sleaze. "I don't know who the hell you are, coming out here when I'm with my girls!"

Water splattered over him and the stranger. Tina and Christine still in their own little world…

But Ben didn't slow down. Too used to this chaos. "But you tell us first, why the hell you're here, buddy?"

Unfazed, the man stole a glance at Patsey. She took an uncomfortable step back upon sight. Her grip growing tighter on the spatula.

"You hear me!" Ben yelled.

The stranger immediately turned his glare toward him. His movements quick and eerie. *Precise.*

"What the hell do you want!" Ben growled.

The stranger just smiled. His white teeth a weapon of their own. "You abused them, didn't you."

Ben glared at him. "What the hell—"

"I know, Ben." The man pointed at the kids. Their loud swimming didn't slow down. Together, they kept making waves in the wading pool. "I know you've abused them their whole fucking lives! I've seen you."

Ben lost his confrontational confidence. Right then and there.

The man leaned in closer toward him, taunting Ben. Zeroing in on his soul. "You touched them, didn't you, Ben? You and Patsey?"

Still holding the beer, Ben couldn't say a word. He joined Patsey's paralyzing paranoia. Not even the constant carefree cries of

Tina and Christine could comfort him from this catatonia. Their splashing and screaming. None of it could rescue him from this creeped-out unease.

Without hesitation, the stranger confronted Patsey. Her restless silence. "Both of you did, didn't you?" he continued in a voice with no hint of accent. Of mercy.

Neither Patsey nor Ben said anything. They couldn't.

Taking a step back, the mysterious man reached behind him. "That's all I needed to know."

Behind them, trailer doors burst open. A chorus of frightened footsteps and Southern sirens surrounded the scene.

They won't matter! thought the stranger. *Just stay focused.*

"What the hell's going on over there, Ben!" a gruff voice barked across the driveway. From a hideous trailer the stranger had no interest in seeing.

The scowl reappeared on Ben's face. A fiery aimed right at the stranger. "You son-of-a-bitch!" he cried. Ben raised the Bud, ready to make his weapon out of that drink of choice.

The man kept his cool. No false move made. He withdrew the Ruger and fired two quick shots at close range.

Patsey screamed as chaos overtook Everett's mobile homes. Her voice louder than the thunderous gunfire. The shot the most excitement these Perry, Florida rejects had seen and felt since the Fourth of July. Only this murder incited horror rather than drunken patriotism.

Ben's corpse fell straight back into the pool. A triumphant *SPLASH* accompanied his dropped beer. The bullets left his face in splattered pieces, his beard thicker with gooey flesh. That belly about to be even more bloated...

Contrasting the rest of the trailer park panic, Tina and Christine still played tag in water quickly turning red. Laughing, they splashed the crimson over one another. Maneuvering around the big, bloody float that was their daddy's dead body.

Christine shoved Tina against the edge of the pool, creating a wave.

"Tag!" Christine teased. "You're it!"

The stranger stared at the kids in disbelief. His face blank but baffled. *They really aren't the smartest.* He watched Tina chase her sister, gaining ground until she ran straight into Ben's floating cadaver! *Goddamn, I didn't know they were this bad.*

"Leave them alone!" Patsey yelled.

The stranger turned his focus toward her.

Glowering, Patsey raised the spatula. "You get the hell outta here!" She pointed the weapon to the rest of Everett's mobile homes. That low-class congregation.

The stranger looked on at his surroundings with cold indifference to spare, his skepticism showing off a smug sarcasm. Even in the face of families watching from afar, of worried voices shouting, of glares across all ages zeroed in on the man. Due to the lack of trees and landscaping, Everett's shotgun layout also showed the stranger a clear view of Mark running toward them. Or running about as well as old his age and intoxication would allow...

"They're already calling the police!" Patsey yelled.

The stranger chuckled.

His calmness unsettled Patsey further. The children's splashes and wading still formed a serene September soundtrack. The sunshine still gorgeous cinematography. But the stranger's arrival had turned this summer daydream into a nightmare beyond Patsey's control.

Mark got closer. His fear well on display. Mark not used to playing hero.

With a cryptic smile, the man watched Mark stumble through a hot, drunken daze.

Mark pointed at him. "Hey now, you leave those kids alone—"

Showing off for the crowd, the man aimed right at Mark, stopping the old man dead in his tracks.

Immediately, Mark threw his hands up.

The stranger's muscles were now all the more clearer, not to mention his steady grip as well. The merciless glare, the beaming eyes. Not even the sweat slowed the intruder down. Nothing could. "Get back!" he commanded.

Mark stopped playing hero right then and there. He turned and ran back to that hideous mobile home. His steps sloppy, his speed only "fast" enough to match his drunken daze.

Everyone else at Everett's kept their distance. They just stood and watched from afar. Watching out of both fear and entertainment. The only confrontations out here usually involved drunk, abusive husbands, drunk, abusive wives, or usually the more common variation: mutual domestic violence. Not too often did a handsome man appear from the heat wielding a loaded gun. Much less actually cross the line from shit talk and weak swings to murder in the first.

The stranger took note of each one of the viewers. Not so much the gun keeping them at bay as his dispassionate scowl. The slight smirk.

"Just leave us alone! Please!" Patsey shouted.

Now the man turned to confront his latest target. His smile gone and replaced by focused fire. An emotion for once started to appear: wrath. Nothing pulled him away now. No Mark. None of Everett's inhabitants, deadbeats, or ex-cons. Not even Tina and Christine's constant movement, the constant waves crashing out the pool, the red water splashing closer to the stranger's sandals.

Patsey's glare grew more intense. A glare in hardened cops and soulless executioners...and somehow one all too common for this twenty-three-year-old. "You heard me!" Exploding, she pointed that spatula down the road! Her roaring rage conflicting the man's controlled anger. "You get the hell outta here! You hear me?"

The stranger took another methodical step. *This is how she really is. Especially when they beat and molested those kids.* "I'm not going anywhere, Patsey Slaughter."

Against Patsey's incensed stare, the man pointed the revolver right at her.

"You son-of-a-bitch!" shouted Patsey's shrill scream.

"You did it to them!" the stranger continued. "Your own daughters. You enjoyed beating them, hurting them! Both of you."

No tears appeared in Patsey's eyes. No sign of remorse. The morbid memories made her more bitter than empathetic. Her rage boiling in the Florida heat, Patsey pointed the spatula at the stranger! "You don't know shit, asshole! The cops are on their way! They'll *fry* you! I'll make goddamn sure of it!"

Still, Christine and Tina went round and round the pool. Around Ben's drenched corpse. Around the standoff involving their mother.

The splashing and cackles didn't faze the man. Nor did Patsey's fury...

"You get your ass off my property!" Patsey yelled.

A look of cold disgust remained on the man's face. Now he was ready to make his move. Holding the Ruger, he marched toward Patsey. The sudden movement scaring her.

Patsey staggered back, her face full of unfamiliar fear. That aggressive combativeness crashing upon seeing the stranger charge toward her. His demeanor at a chilling calm. His pace precise, his strides strong. His hunt *too* perfect. A *robotic* execution.

The stranger got nearer, his gun at the ready. Staring down Patsey as much as the man's unblinking eyes.

Adrenaline mixing with the nerves, Patsey stole a look at her daughters. They kept laughing in the September sun. Christine now with her arms wrapped around Ben's neck, her obese size sending her daddy's dead weight sinking straight down.

Patsey saw the stranger stop a few feet away. He aimed right at her pale face.

A *BURST OF FLAMES* startled her. Patsey turned back to see a small fire spread across the grill. Over the burgers, over the rust. The flames matching her internal temper and external rage. "No!" she yelled. Hoisting her spatula, Patsey confronted the man. The face of a mom gone psycho. Not so much defending her children as her turf. "Get outta here!"

For once, the stranger hesitated. Fear hit him but not enough to dare show it. *Now she looks crazy…scary.*

With a rebel yell, Patsey ran toward him. Her Southern siren hitting an animalistic apex, her large frame and flowing sweat mirroring that of a wild predator on the prowl.

Regaining his confident control, the stranger fired away. Three bullets stormed out.

Two hit Patsey's chest. One right between the eyes.

Enough of an impact to bring this beast down.

Patsey collapsed to the ground, right there in her front yard. The gooey crater in her head struck red oil. Blood spread across the brunette's lifeless body, doing everyone a favor and turning that bikini into a wide crimson dress.

The spatula lay at her fingertips, the bright sunshine reflecting off its glistening metal.

Unusual silence sunk into Everett's. The simultaneously nosy and horrified neighbors were long gone. The bystanders chased inside not by threat but death. Mark long gone by now...

Everything was quiet save for the splashes. The giggling. Not even two murders could slow down Ben and Patsey's daughters. If it wasn't clear by the way they played with their daddy's dead body, the girls' lack of development certainly was now. Little did they know this would be the last game of tag they'd ever have at the shit trailer park. But they were damn sure enjoying it.

The smell of smoke joined the humidity. Not to mention the nauseating stench of slaughter. But none of it bothered the stranger, not at this point in his personal mission.

He turned and looked across the street. To the forest from which he came. Where he left behind both his cell phone and journal.

Now the hard part, his melancholy realized. Forcing a cold stare over what was a stifling sympathy, he turned his attention to the little girls.

The man's steps were soft and steady. Tina and Christine didn't even notice when he stopped right beside the pool. They never took note of his piercing eyes or revolver. Nor did they stop when he pointed that Ruger right at them.

"Come with me, Christine," the stranger said, that clinical tone of origins unknown.

Now the two girls stood in the red water, clueless rather than confused. Their sloppy smiles remained.

The man reached toward Christine's chubby arm. His movements soft and calm. "We're just gonna play inside, alright."

"Okay," Christine squeaked. Then, with excitement to spare, she grabbed hold of the stranger's hand. Pieces of Ben's grey matter sticking straight into his palm.

But the man didn't flinch. He went along with it. *God help them*. The stranger helped Christine out of the pool. "We'll play hide-and-seek," he reassured.

Tina threw up her arms, splashing more blood water. "But what about me?"

With Christine at his side, the man smiled at her eight-year-old sister. His grin weak and weary. His canvas struggling to stay blank…struggling to hide the looming dread…the nerves. "We're gonna go hide." With a trembling hand, he waved the revolver toward Tina. "So you just stay there. Count to sixty, and when you're done," he motioned the Ruger at the pathetic trailer, "you come inside and find us."

Christine jumped up and down. "Okay! Yay!"

Feeling her childhood joy only further unsettled the stranger. *Just be glad the glasses hide the tears you can't.*

Laughing, Tina waded over toward the other side. "Okay!" She pushed Ben's body away. Eager to play.

"You better keep your eyes closed!" Christine teased Tina.

Tina crashed against the edge, rattling the entire pool. The choppy water toying with her father's corpse. Tina turned away from the man and her sister. "I ain't cheating!" With that, she jammed her hands over her eyes. "One! Two! Three!" shrieked the countdown.

Caught up in the thrill of the game, Christine pulled the stranger toward the trailer. The power well beyond her youth. "C'mon, let's hide!"

Together, they stumbled through the soggy soil. Christine leading the charge onto that rickety wooden porch. All while only her sister's voice followed them...

The sweltering Perry heat didn't bother the man, but the girls' innocence did. Especially Christine's. *Just remember. Remember what she'll become. A monster.*

Christine slammed open the screen door. Turned the loose knob.

A chorus of cheap fans greeted them. A living room populated by torn furniture, scattered beer bottles, snack wrappers, and roaches.

"Fifteen, sixteen!" continued Tina.

With a big smile, Christine confronted the man, one hand covering the side of her mouth. "Let's go in the kitchen!" said her not-so-discreet whisper.

The stranger clung tighter to his gun. Desperate to hold on to it amidst the sweat. Amidst the guilt. *Remember what she'll do,* he reminded himself. He forced a soothing smile on the young girl. "That's a good idea. Let's go."

"Twenty! Twenty-one!" said Tina's Southern shriek.

Christine turned and looked toward her. "No cheating, Tina!"

Preparing for the painful process, the man readjusted his glasses.

"I'm not!" Tina shouted back. "Twenty-four! Twenty-five!"

The stranger grabbed hold of Christine's hand. Still, a soft grip, if a bit more rigid. Forceful.

Christine faced his stoic stone face.

"Why don't you show me where the kitchen is?" he asked her.

Christine's smile only got wider and wackier. Carefree to the extreme. "Okay!"

"Alright." The man started to step inside.

Christine held him back. Her massive body an anchor for the front porch.

"Forty! Forty-one!" went the other child's countdown.

The man looked into Christine's elated expression. This portrait of an overjoyed young girl. One oblivious to the horror around her…and awaiting her.

"What's your name, mister?" she asked, her cute twang full of curiosity.

Amused, the man gave her a soulful grin. A rare emotional tell. "Kevin."

Still beaming, Christine hesitated, a playful pending of approval.

"Forty-four! Forty-five!" continued her sister. "I'm almost there!"

"Okay, Mr. Kevin," Christine said. Her quick footsteps tortured the creaking porch. "I like you! Let's go!"

All Kevin could do was nod and follow. No words escaped him. None that wouldn't give away the sadness squeezing his soul.

"Forty-nine! Fifty!" Tina shouted.

Kevin let Christine pull him inside. The Ruger started to shake in his hand. The insurmountable dread piling up. Once Christine slammed the door behind them, the immediacy of this macabre moment hit him.

"Hurry!" Christine said.

"Okay," Kevin said, keeping his voice steady. The dark room helped him shield his conflicted conscience. In this profession, you couldn't show weakness, after all. Certainly no empathy.

Remember, Kevin. She kills children. Babies. Christine Falling is a serial killer.

"Fifty-three!" he heard Tina scream out.

Kevin's glower returned. He squeezed the revolver, reaffirming his grip. Then did the same to Christine's hand.

"C'mon!" Christine yelled.

"Fifty-eight! Fifty-nine!" blared the countdown.

Like a panicking soldier, Christine led Kevin through this hideous battlefield. Straight toward a cluttered kitchen.

*

Outside, Tina leaned across the pool's edge. Her hands over her eyes. The forthcoming hunt exciting her into levels of euphoria one could only get at her age…all while Ben's water-logged body floated just a few feet away.

Ann was lying by the grill. She and her husband formed a makeshift Everett's cemetery…

"Sixty!" Tina finished. She opened her eyes and confronted the trailer, the excitement at a frenetic peak. "Ready or not, here I come!"

A single gunshot shattered the start of this childhood tradition. The sound definite enough to echo throughout the empty trailer park.

Tina looked on, stunned. Transfixed to hear that noise coming from inside her own home. For the first time, she could put the pieces together…but only when it involved her kid sister.

An unsettling silence settled upon the scene. Now Tina got chills amidst the ninety-degree weather and blood-warm water. The gallons of tears unable to ever cool her down.

Sure, she didn't know for sure Christine was dead. But deep down, Tina's primitive intuition took over. Regardless of her infantile intellect, the tragedy struck Tina to the core. She knew playtime was over. Forever.

Bawling, Tina staggered out the pool. Blood dripped off her shivering skin. She was all alone with no parent to run to. No sibling to lean on. "Christine!" she yelled.

Only one sound drowned out her anguished cries…the sound of multiple police sirens pulling right into Everett's.

Chapter 2

December 10, 1951

I've been sent back in time to kill bad people. And *only* the bad.

No, I'm not being forced against my will. I'm just doing what's best for my country. What's best for all of us.

The technology where I'm from lets me leap through time. Through different eras. The assignments vary. All I get is the name, location, and proof of what crimes they committed in their lifetime. And then comes the simple part: extinguishing the evil. Wipe it from history before it ever happens.

The list goes on, but so far, I've yet to witness any butterfly effect. Yet to see what my "missions" have led to in the current year. Right now, I just stay focused on the task at hand. Ridding the world of its all-time monsters one at a time.

Like a routine morning, such is the speed and spontaneity with which I wake up to a new setting. This one a cold December afternoon. I stumble around the middle of a forest. Past a few clearings. A few campsites. My jeans and green jacket battered by the biting wind.

I stole a look at my phone. The GPS said I was getting closer.

Finally, I stop and see it: a red Chevy parked about twenty feet away. A two-lane highway lurking beyond the pickup.

Hesitant, I readjusted my glasses. Felt sweat drench my curly blonde hair. Felt the dread building up inside me. But I had to face these fears…Again.

I took a deep breath. Pulled the pistol out of my pocket, its silencer already attached. The gun's cold metal uncomfortable in my trembling touch.

Then I marched onward. Discreet but quick for this ambush.

Glancing all around me, I saw nothing. No one out here but the targets and I. The nearby highway so lonely. The forest a cemetery ready for its inaugural grave.

The closer I got, the more I could see how old the car's style was. A 1952 Chevy. And then I saw wild movement shake it. Heard desperate cries coming from inside.

I clenched the gun tighter. Lunged toward the window on the driver's side.

And there was the evil.

A chubby nine-year-old boy sat in the passenger's seat. A small backpack at his feet. The boy's round face beyond nervous. His body shaking in the flannel shirt.

Behind the wheel, a tall man leaned back. He was even chubbier than the boy. A dark fedora rested on his head. The man's excitement contrasting the kid's timid hesitation. His smile growing wider as he unbuckled his khakis.

Paralyzed by nerves, the kid stayed back. His eyes stayed on the man's crotch. But he never once moved.

The man waved the boy in closer. He was ready to lower his underwear, his spirits jolly for this most disturbing act.

Then I made my move. Using the pistol, I tapped on the window.

Startled, both the man and boy faced the gun. They panicked.

In a burst, the little boy snatched his backpack and threw open the door.

The man struggled to slide his pants back on. He yelled at the boy.

But the kid wasn't gonna listen. In mere seconds, he was out of the truck. Ran straight into the forest.

I banged on the window once more.

With the man's attention, I pointed the pistol down.

His perverse pleasure fading, the man lowered the window. Now I was face to face with the pedo. He scanned my muscular frame. His weak white smile and baby blues having no effect on my anger. My duty.

"Is something the matter?" the man asked in a raspy Chicago accent.

"Yeah," I responded. I put the gun to his head. "You.

Behind a cold glare, I pulled the trigger. The top of the man's head exploded. Like confetti, blood, gray matter, and fedora pieces scattered everywhere. The Chevy became a messy mausoleum.

The man's corpse fell into the passenger's seat. A bleeding crater stuck in his forehead. The pedo's khakis still unbuckled. His blank eyes looking straight up. A body forever preserved in its sickening final few moments.

Holding the gun, I walked off toward the woods. Off to where I last saw the boy. The young victim.

I folded my arms to stay warm. Somehow, the afternoon got colder. Especially the further I journeyed through those deep, dark woods.

Up ahead, I saw the boy in a clearing. The chubby kid turned around to face me. His body shivering. Tears in his eyes.

Staying calm, I jammed the pistol in my pocket. "Hey, it's okay!" I said.

I leaned down in front of him. The kid more vulnerable all alone. Even with no big bad wolf preying on him.

"I'm sorry," I said, keeping my voice gentle. "I didn't mean to scare you."

"What happened?" the boy said. Anxiety conquered his dark eyes. "What are you gonna do?"

With a reassuring touch, I placed my hands on his shoulders. "It's okay," I said. I squeezed tighter. "I'm just here to help. That's all."

The kid hugged me. His weight almost knocked me back, his strength quite surprising. But his tears only accelerated. As did his sympathetic breakdown. "I didn't do anything!" he cried. "I didn't want to! I didn't!"

Like a loving parent, I rubbed his back. "I know, son," I said. "It's not your fault."

I pulled him back, making him face me. "I just want to help," I told the boy. "That's why I'm here."

We were out there in the eerie wilderness, the boy struggling to speak.

"Hey, mister," he finally said. "I'm sorry."

Uneasy, I stared at him. "What do you mean?" I asked. Then I saw what lurked behind him. Toward the darkness on the edge of this clearing. In those woods.

"About what I did," the boy said.

Ten feet away, I saw his unzipped backpack lying on the ground. Right next to a couple of charred turkeys. Each of them burnt alive. Their eyes bulging. Their dead tongues hanging out amidst a final gasp for life. One of the turkeys' corpses still twitching in a helpless postmortem rhythm.

The weapons were unusual but effective. Tattered balloons. Each of them filled to the brim with gasoline by the boy.

"I just couldn't help it, mister," I heard the kid say, his voice simultaneously innocent and tormented.

My horrified gaze drifted down to his fingers. To the box of matches lying beside him. Five of them were freshly struck. The kid had an executioner's touch at the age of nine.

"I had to do something," the kid confessed through the waterfall of tears. "I couldn't do it anymore!"

Weeping, I faced him. Caressed his pudgy face. "I know, John."

The boy's eyes grew bigger. Bewildered beyond belief. "How did you know my name?"

I didn't answer. Instead, I gripped his shoulder as I stood up. "Just come with me, John. Let's get out of here."

Wiping away his tears, John let me lead us back through the woods. Past the turkeys. Past one of his very first crime scenes.

I patted the kid on the shoulder. "You'll be fine. I promise."

He gave me a weak smile. "What's your name, mister?"

"Kevin," I said. "And just remember, I'm only here to help you, John."

Deeper in the forest, I didn't bother holding back the tears. Didn't bother suppressing my shivers as my hand reached into the hoodie pocket. For the gun. "I'm taking you to a better place," I reassured the boy.

1951 never felt colder. I couldn't even blame the snow since there wasn't any in Chicago that day. Only the chilling company I made. The looming execution of one John Wayne Gacy. A portrait of a serial killer at a young age I had to erase. Bundy was tough, but this would be even tougher. Even more tragic.

After all, the ages were the most challenging part of the missions. Not executing evil, but having to do so before they reached their malevolent peak. When they were just children.

Chapter 3

October 22, 1929

There wasn't much downtime when you worked for The Retroactive Project. My bosses watched the jobs. The assignments one after the other. And thanks to mankind, there was never a shortage of targets.

The 2040 committee better be glad I was both qualified and dumb enough to enlist. Certainly, there weren't many others wanting to in this post-COVID-19 harmony. None as reliable as me, at least…

After a few days of recovery, I got dropped further back in the terrifying past. Into a bygone era even more primitive and savage than modern times.

1929 was one of America's scariest years. There was the obvious chaos and panic of The Great Depression and Stock Market Crash here in the States. But these historical footnotes offered us a more hidden horror: serial killers. Psychos before the term got popular.

They've always been around. Men, women, young, old, it didn't matter. They've always lurked in the shadows. It's just only recently we've given them a spotlight. Not to mention a camera and microphone. An *audience*.

But mass murders didn't quite have that notoriety in 1929 Arkansas. Hell, they weren't even called serial killers back then. But that still didn't stop the Retroactive from sending me out here to stop one.

I did what I was told and dressed for the era in a white undershirt and loose brown slacks. My hair slicked back with copious amounts of mousse. The cell phone hidden in my back pocket, the Luger pistol tucked into my waistband.

I stepped foot into a cold October morning. Graysonia, Arkansas my location. Unprepared for the chilling wind, I journeyed through the wilderness. This roaring forest of tall trees and wildflowers. The ground nothing but smooth grass. The Ozarks this wasn't. Graysonia a smaller rural town, and by now, I was far off the beaten path. The cabins and mobile homes grew few and far between. If not for the bitter cold and eerie isolation, I'd have found the scene pretty. Peaceful if not for the trying task I had. The duty filling my subconscious with dread.

Beneath a gray morning, I marched onward, past clusters of purple beautyberries and against the crows' haunting chorus. Graysonia like a national park that transcended time. A cute little area that was also only twenty years away from becoming a forgotten ghost town.

From what I saw, the Crash affected nothing out here. Houses were always poor, civilization and commerce sparse as is. Not a car was in sight. No electricity. A stray pond the only pool in these parts. Sure, I didn't expect The Roaring Twenties (obvious enough by my working-class wardrobe), but now I feared I'd overdressed for what was a snapshot of late-nineteenth-century poverty. The people around here too impoverished to even afford sharecroppers. Not that there were many profitable crops out here, to begin with. This setting a long way away from the gaudy luxury of Zelda and F. Scott Fitzgerald and their fellow Stratford-on-Odeon crew.

The farther I traveled, the colder it got. These Arkansas woods were endless. For awhile there, I felt maybe they'd given me the wrong instructions. That the Retroactive had made an unusual mistake in leading me down this journey into an Arctic Hell. The undershirt definitely a miscalculation on their part. Our meteorologist was still terrible even with 2040 technology.

Then I heard a familiar sound. One that'd draw a smile from most but only a crippling unease in me. The sound of a young boy making construction noises. Sledgehammers, screwdrivers, sawing. And of course, the innocent imitation of a roaring car.

I reached a small clearing. A front-row seat to an All-American boy crouched down all alone. An eleven-year-old with short dark hair. Wearing a clean red tee shirt. His jeans neat and unwrinkled. First day of school clothes.

Excited, the kid kept alternating between those many city noises. Not playing with toys but an assortment of leaves, sticks, straw, and other natural resources. A Great Depression playset.

"Then we'll put you right here!" said his soft tone. The young man positioned a stick on top of two rocks. A precise touch.

"Like that!" He pulled his hand back slowly, admiring that Arkansas bridge he built from literal scratch. "There you go, Mr. Mayor," he said in a humorous attempt at a deep masculine tone. "There's your new bridge to Graysonia!" He reached for a few more rocks. "We'll get to work on those skyscrapers!" continued his cute voice.

I stood still, intrigued. Watching Mack Ray Edwards continue his architectural mastery. The kid decades away from beginning his demented killing spree...his *child*-killing spree. Several of those future victims younger than he was right now. Their bodies left under the freeways he'd later help build.

Regardless of the horror, I felt the empathy I forced myself to suppress...struggled to suppress. How could someone like Edwards progress from here to psychopath?

The boy now stacked rocks and sticks together, forming makeshift floors. The biggest building in the history of Graysonia. His noises the only soundtrack he needed for his imaginary success. The intelligence, a maturity for his age well on display. And judging by the clothes, the kid had folks who cared. Or at least had money.

Folding my arms, I did the mental prep. Fought the cold and guilt. I took one deep breath, then approached the young Mack.

"Hey there," I said, my voice deep but friendly.

Mack looked up at me. Not scared. He had a rock in one hand, a twig in the other. His calm expression like a shopkeeper's when greeted by a customer.

Grinning, I pointed toward his model city. "Hey, that's pretty nice."

"Thanks, mister," Mack said in a low, unrattled voice. Back to work, he stacked the "tools" onto that developing second floor.

I knelt beside him. The smile still there. My hand nowhere near the Luger...unable to hide my heart. "Do you come here often?"

Not missing a beat, Mack grabbed another rock. "Uh-huh."

Leaning in closer, I pointed toward that skyscraper. "You need any help with that?"

Mack looked over at me, surprised by my offer, the joy obvious in his narrow eyes.

No wonder he reacted so calmly. There was no reason to be scared when I was what his loneliness wanted: someone to play with.

A big grin dominated Mack's face. "Yeah!" He waved a bony hand toward a stack of small twigs. "Grab those, and we'll make it bigger!"

I chuckled. "Alright." I looked over at our tools for the trade. No longer shivering. "Let's do it."

*

Fifteen minutes later, we'd finished that second floor: the detail, the design, all of it well executed by Mack.

We shot the breeze throughout our hard work, reaffirming what I was already told about this serial killer as a young man.

Decent family, intelligent, an uncanny ability to "fit in." But still, I enjoyed every second. The kid's answers were quick but sincere. He even told me he appreciated the help.

The weather never got better. There was still a harsh chill around us, still silence save for the crows' creepy calls. But now I was comfortable. Moments like these, this bonding, were a welcome sight from the Retroactive lifestyle. That constant clinical cynicism. In Graysonia, I didn't have to be bombarded with morbid info or commanded to kill children. I could just help build an imaginary town. Actually talk to someone on a human level, even if it was one of my targets.

In the back of my mind, the unease loomed. I knew I couldn't stay in 1929 forever. All the work I spent building this friendship would be brief before ending in bloodshed. There was no turning back on these serial killers, not if I didn't want to jeopardize my own life. That is *our* world in 2040.

Yet, I was still tempted. Swayed by my biggest weakness: sympathy. Mack was interesting. He was different and innovative. Articulate for his age. And honestly, I enjoyed getting to know him. I was *glad* to finally have a chance encounter built not on instant murder and confrontation but on something friendly. After all, could an eleven-year-old really be this manipulative? This *sociopathic*?

This truth bothered me. Because I didn't wanna believe it. I couldn't...

Especially once Mack grabbed my hand, Hhs grip electric and elated.

"Can you walk me home?" he asked.

I nodded. "Yeah. Of course."

Mack waved toward the "city." "We did a good job, didn't we?"

With a father's pride, I smiled at the sight. Our own miniature Utopia. "Damn sure did."

"We can work on it later!" The boy then stood up, making me take his lead. "I just gotta see Mom and Daddy. It's lunchtime!"

"I understand."

Mack pulled me away from the clearing. Back into that fucking forest.

The harsh wind returned. As did my October chills. And with it came the pressing task. The painful task. I looked all around the towering oaks and outright isolation. What we were on was barely a path. Certainly one only occupied by Mack and his family. But it was ripe for the Retroactive. To my horror, I realized it was perfect for the kill. The time was now…

"Mama's cooking fried chicken today!" Mack beamed.

I let him drag me further within those woods. The area got darker. And so did my dread.

"It's my favorite!" Mack's innocence continued.

Overhead, trees blocked out more of whatever weak light the overcast sky had to offer. The crows' chorus became louder.

Mack stole a smile at me. "You know Halloween's coming up, dontcha?"

"Yeah," I stuttered.

"I'm gonna be an Army fighter! Daddy's helping me with the costume!"

Battling the emotions, my other hand slipped on over to the Luger. Little did my new friend know he'd never get a bite of his mama's beloved chicken. Or that he was leading me straight to his grave...

"That sounds good, Mack," I said.

The boy came to a sudden stop. There in this daytime heart of darkness, he turned and looked at me, his face full of fear, his grip turning cold.

I just stared on at the fright. Not that I could blame him. I recognized his horrifying epiphany. And behind the glasses and forced detachment, I was sure he could recognize mine.

"How did you know my name?" Mack asked, his voice at its lowest and most vulnerable.

Not saying a word, I stole another look all around us, making sure we were alone. But also because I could no longer face the kid. Face our fatal friendship.

Dropping my hand, Mack staggered back. "I didn't tell you my name..."

He's a serial killer, I tried reminding myself. I tried to remember the evil. The *future* evil. Finally, I confronted Mack Ray

Edwards. "I know who you are, Mack," I said, keeping my voice steady and soulless. The executioner's poise I'd had preached into me. Seeing Mack shiver before me, I retrieved the pistol. "And I know what you become."

Reserves of horror hit the boy. Only he didn't cry. In fact, he couldn't take his eyes off me. He couldn't move. Mack was a scared statue.

In the cold, I pointed the pistol right at him. Usually, this was quick. Painless. The whole brutal process was really. I didn't say much. I just exterminated evil. But for the first time, I was supposed to kill a target I'd spent time talking to. That I bonded with. Always a big no-no to the Retroactive…but I couldn't help it. The loneliness got to me. I knew Mack could relate.

"Please, mister!" Mack whimpered. He took another step back, not even flinching when his shoe snapped a twig.

The wind made the gun shake in my hand. Or at least, I blamed the wind. The inner torment just intensified. I let the guilt consume my soul. Felt tears well up. Now here I was being the scared child. "I have to," I stated, barely burying the raw empathy. "It's for your own good, Mack." I got ready to pull the trigger. Ready to fire a shot into this psycho's Halloween costume: that of a cute, charming young boy.

But I couldn't. Not this up close and personal. Not when staring down that innocent face. The "killer" shivering and bracing for that fatal bullet. So vulnerable and far from the monster he'd become…

Breathing out cold air, I slightly lowered the Luger. My soul and brain at war. "I'm sorry—"

Mack sensed his chance. Acting off shrewd instincts, he turned and hauled ass through the woods.

"Shit!" I cried. Even in this internal struggle, I knew my responsibility. What I had to do. Not to mention what the Retroactive would do to me if I fucked this up. If Mack Ray Edwards got away or if I accidentally killed an "innocent," I'd face consequences. And worst of all, confront my own tortured subconscious. Particularly if I let the boy survive and grow up to become the serial killer he was destined to be. Then I'd be the one at fault for those six or more victims.

The kid was quick. But I'd had training. The military service paid off for times like these when shit hit the fan.

I gained ground there in the forest. Stomping on scattered sticks, pushing aside dangling branches. I was no longer cold thanks to the adrenaline and sweat. still clinging to that gun.

Mack led me down this spiraling, secluded path. His red shirt a moving target I struggled to aim at.

Gasping for breath, I didn't slow down. Not even when sweat whipped across my glasses like Arkansas raindrops.

This green wasteland was endless. And Mack knew it way better than me. His elusiveness already on display, a trait that'd help him evade police for decades. Yet, I got closer and closer. My sympathy held at bay by the panic. The urgency to stop a killer.

"Mack!" I cried.

He just flashed me a cold glare. Hatred rather than horror in the eleven-year-old's expression.

Suddenly, I stumbled into a tower of rocks and tree limbs, knocking them all over! One of Mack's "buildings" now reduced to rubble. I stole a glance at the debris, the pieces resembling a ritualistic design. But hearing Mack's frenetic footsteps, I knew I couldn't play surveyor for long!

I forced myself to run a few yards more, the distance between Mack and I closing slowly but surely. Kids were always the toughest to chase down, after all. And in my expert opinion, they seemed to have a hell of a lot more energy when they were cold-blooded murderers.

Fighting the fatigue, I raised the pistol. My legs, my entire body, running on empty. But so was the boy's. *Keep going, Kevin! He's a killer!*

Excitement exhilarated me. I saw the finish line: a clearing Mack was about to enter. Fewer trees, less wilderness. *Faint* light finally.

Mack ran into the spot. Myself not far behind.

Here's his grave, I thought, a desperate attempt to play tough. Or at least fool myself into feeling no remorse for gunning down a child.

Just as I rushed into the clearing, the surroundings came into view, a *literal* change of scenery. I stopped and scanned the scene. The trimmed grass was only a part of this perfect front lawn. The isolated wooden cabin stood about twenty feet away. Mack Ray Edwards's childhood home.

I felt warmer in this Great Depression attempt at the American Dream. The cabin featured rocking chairs and a glorious chimney. A pretty pastoral portrait this house was. And throughout the front yard, I saw Mack's fingerprints on more of those homemade buildings and bridges. The architecture embellished with hand-carved pieces of wood and torn cloth.

Mack ran straight for the front door. Straight to the parents who did their damndest to raise him well.

Do or die, Kevin. I glanced back at the forest. Toward the constant crows. Now I had to finish off the killer…the boy.

"Mom!" I heard Mack scream.

Restraining the guilt I felt and would forever feel, I faced the boy and aimed. I was one of the best shots in my squad. When I had the time, I couldn't miss, and today was no different.

The first shot hit Mack's leg. Enough to get what I reminded myself was a future serial killer down.

"No! Mama!" Mack screamed. His small hands cradled the vicious wound. The buckets of blood streaming around the bullet.

Mack's shrill, vulnerable cries shook me to the core. His weeping would go on to haunt me, but I couldn't let them right now. Not for this execution.

The brutal chills came back. That ominous October weather. The overwhelming sadness inside me.

Like a hurt child on the playground, Mack leaned up on the ground. The tears and screaming constant. A pathetic recreation of a soldier on the battlefield. One so helpless and alone that I realized Mack didn't need that Army costume right now.

He's a murderer, Kevin, I reminded myself. *This isn't who he really is. What he becomes.* I took a deep breath and pulled the trigger.

The kill shot was fast. Mack's death happened before I could even react. Before I could feel my conscience morph into melancholia.

There Mack lay on the lawn in a burgeoning pool of blood. The young man's forehead excavated by a single slug from this Luger. The scattered make-believe skyscrapers his funeral candles.

At least, he was at peace. That's all I could tell myself. A mercy kill on all fronts…a necessary sacrifice.

I lowered the Luger. No longer able to keep the tears suppressed, I let that weep flag fly. My body shivered beneath the Brando undershirt. The mousse dying beneath layers of sweat. The tears falling behind my glasses.

"Hey!" bellowed a voice of Southern rage.

Startled, I looked off toward the cabin, that cozy country home.

I locked eyes with Hellfire and brimstone. Mack's tall and lanky dad. But what was also one concerned father, an unusual sight for my line of work.

Disturbed, the dad marched past the rocking chairs. His eyes full of tears, his face full of rage. "You son-of-a-bitch!" he hurled at me. "You killed my son!"

The fear froze me. Not to mention the rising guilt.

"What the hell'd you do to him?" Mack's father shouted, shredding his emotions in a painful purge. He staggered off the porch in those jeans and heavy jacket. The weeping unable to stave off the anger. Unable to keep him from getting a clearer view of me.

But still, I didn't move. The murder weapon stayed in my hand. The sorrow stayed in my soul. I could not even contemplate escape until I saw Mack's mom emerge from behind that front door. A pretty young woman not even in her thirties and already the distraught mother of a murdered child.

She broke down in tears, immediately collapsing next to a rocking chair, her sobs uncontained.

I knew then that I couldn't wait around. Not from fear of the father's fiery but out of the overwhelming sadness of it all. The sympathy I had for these parents. Not that I could relate. Just grieve.

As Mack's dad charged toward me, I turned and disappeared inside the forest. Right back where I came from. Where I first encountered Mack Ray Edwards.

Why would I talk to his devastated parents? What could I explain? How could I tell them what their son would become *regardless* of how great they were? Of how much they loved him. No matter what, Mack would become a disturbed serial killer. One who'd murder kids. I couldn't explain what even science couldn't understand. What the rational, empathetic human mind couldn't comprehend. The type of unnerving horror, not even the Retroactive had figured out over a century later.

To my relief, I managed to escape Graysonia and that ordeal. I never had to confront Mack's parents. Just pity the pain they felt. That *understandable* pain any parent would feel in the same situation.

That fateful morning in Arkansas stuck with me. Not just because of the bond I had with Mack Edwards before exterminating him, but because of the first close call I'd had with any parents. And for the first time, I had witnesses to my "murder."

Curiosity compelling me, I read the newspaper articles from the Arkansas press in that era. My "murder" even reached the *Arkansas Democrat-Gazette*. The articles were all the same, even as the years went by. As the decades passed. Mack Ray Edwards being gunned down remained one of the creepiest cold cases in the state's history. And the police never had a suspect. Instead, they just had that description the boy's mother and father gave them: that of a handsome middle-aged man with curly blonde hair and big glasses. A man they'd never seen before. With a motive and origins unknown. A perfect stranger.

Chapter 4

The Taylor County Police Department was an outdated building even by 1970s standards. Trapped in Perry, Florida's decrepit downtown district, TCPD was a brick eyesore somehow still standing for well over fifty years. Aside from a lazy sheriff in Tommy Loomis, the department hosted a handful of deputies, detectives, and holding cells.

There weren't many windows. Not that they were needed considering the lack of life both inside and out. This part of downtown had no pretty square, only abandoned businesses, and the few homeless not living at Everett's left wandering the quiet streets. Perry was a peaceful town, after all. Some would say boring. That is until TCPD got those panicked phone calls coming in from Everett's Mobile Home Parks of all places. Not for DV or drunken brawls. Not for the usual but something more serious. Something scary.

For once, this sleepy little town had some excitement, only in the disturbing form: three murders in one day. Nearly the entire Slaughter family wiped out in one attack. The mother, father, and a young daughter all gunned down. The police and neighbors saw no motive. Especially for why their killer let the oldest daughter Tina live…

Sure, Ben and Patsey were disliked. The whole family was nothing more than trailer trash, after all. A fixture for the drunken drama and family dysfunction the city did its best to contain at Everett's. But murder wasn't the norm around here.

At the center of the mystery was the stranger who called himself Kevin. The suspect who dropped the murder weapon and turned himself in the second police arrived.

There in the heat, amidst Tina's painful sobs and the neighbors' nosy cries, Kevin let the cops cuff him with no fight. His face a blank canvas.

No one knew who the hell he was. No one had ever seen him before in these parts. The man had no license. No identification. Aside from the era-appropriate fashion and Ruger pistol, his mannerisms and voice felt out of place. Out of time.

Regardless of Kevin's cold calmness, everyone felt stifling unease around him. Then again, the locals were always icy around a Perry outsider. Much less a murderer.

Thankfully for Sheriff Loomis and Mayor Jennifer Hunter, this was 1970, and in the middle of a Florida Panhandle not many people cared about. The press wasn't on them yet. After all, nobody cared about the Slaughters, not even in their own hometown.

On this scorching September day, TCPD had time to dig into Kevin before the media could. Before this town of seven thousand could turn into a shitshow.

Already there was Deputy Gerard John Schaefer assigned to the case. Tall and muscular, Schaefer was rising through the department's ranks at a rapid pace. And at just twenty-four years old, he'd become Sheriff Loomis's most trusted deputy. No easy task for a young man born into Deep South poverty and an abusive, uncaring father.

Now his biggest assignment yet had arrived: joining Detective Sarah Barlow for interviewing Kevin. And on Schaefer's biggest stage yet: the department's best interrogation room. The only one with a working A/C.

Not that Sarah's office was any better. The old building wasn't noteworthy enough for historical preservation. Instead, it was destined for extinction by way of lack of funds. Lack of action.

Sarah made do in her cluttered claustrophobia. Sitting in a wooden chair, she hunched over the dilapidated desk under the dim lights. At the moment, nothing distracted her. Not the lone window, the bland basic clock, the boxes of dusty old files. With the door shut, all she heard was the portable fan's noisy rotation. Detective Barlow immersed in one of the items recovered near the crime scene, an item shown to police by the stranger himself: Kevin's journal.

Sarah had long unbuckled the pristine leather-bound book. She was the first and only person in the Taylor County Police Department to read it thus far…or at least get through those first few entries.

The accounts on John Wayne Gacy and Mack Ray Edwards disturbed her. The handwriting done with a permanent, precise pen. The words conveyed with conviction. These stories involved a man killing innocent children Sarah had never heard of. His reasoning built off a twisted sense of justice. Off "orders" from the future.

Even more unsettling were the many notes scribbled along the margins. On the far corners of this transcribing of thoughts. Scattered words from a stream of consciousness both crazy and consumed by these "missions."

So many more names listed. So many more accounts that couldn't fit in one journal. And deep within Sarah's disturbed intuition, she knew this meant there were many more murders...

But the "diary" wasn't the only thing police found. Kevin's wardrobe and headband fit the 1970 zeitgeist. The counterculture fashion. But that small portable device Kevin claimed was a miniature phone (or a "cell phone" as he called it) didn't.

Still in evidence, no one had tried operating it yet. The fingerprints were valuable, sure. But to TCPD, the risk was too great. No one knew the device's mysterious capabilities. Gerard even suspected it was a bomb.

He's gotta have schizophrenia, was all Sarah could think regarding Kevin. *There's nothing sane about him. He actually believes this shit.*

Leaning back, Sarah swiped her curly bangs aside. By now used to the sweat clinging to her dark brown skin and currently sticking to her navy blue pantsuit. Even with the jacket draped over the chair, there was no escaping this Florida furnace.

A dread stayed inside Sarah. A lingering worry building up behind an angular face that rarely saw sleep. To Sarah, the journals *felt* real, and what unsettled her more was that her instincts were usually correct.

Then again, they had to be. How else could a black single mother in her early thirties work her way up to Lead Detective in 1970s Deep South? Especially in a small town like Perry. Hopefully, this was just Sarah's first step toward working her way back to her more cultured (and more exciting) hometown in Tampa. And a case as strange and eerie as the Slaughter family slayings would go a long way to bringing her the credibility and honor she long deserved. She damn sure was dedicated. Already Sarah's dreams had cost her an ex, her optimism, and her family. But this was Sarah's passion. She couldn't give up now.

That latest scribbled date stared back at her: *October 22, 1929*. The date taunting her with its bizarre possibilities...with Kevin's convincing reality.

Sarah shook her head in disbelief. *It's crazy. He's crazy.* She confronted her crowded desk. The cluster of notes, files, and paperwork. The *layers* of it. A demoralizing sight save for the one clear spot in this inferno: a picture frame showcasing Sarah with her young son Brandon out at Rosehead Park. The five-year-old struck a soulful pose next to his smiling mother. He inherited her scrawny frame, not to mention her observant personality.

In the office, Sarah's reflective smile was only momentary. Then the anxiety kicked in.

It could've been him, she thought. *What if he had killed Brandon?*

Lost in a mind molded by police work and heartbreak, Sarah confronted the journal. She then skimmed through the pages, seeing the many more entries awaiting her. *The many more murders.*

"Jesus fucking Christ," Sarah muttered.

A knock hit the door.

Startled, Sarah faced it. "Yes?"

Gerard stepped inside, his All-American face greeting the detective. The chiseled good looks captured in a tight police uniform. "You ready?"

Sarah grabbed the journal. "Uh, yeah." She stood up. "Let's go."

With a sly smirk, Gerard nodded at the diary. "You really believe all that time travel crap?"

Sarah followed him out into the stifling hallway. Out there, other sweaty cops and detectives were pacing about, not stressed from the sensational murders but the need to hear more. The gossip and speculation a focal point for this high school precinct. "Well, it's one hell of a story." Sarah closed her office door.

"Aw, it's the usual psychobabble bullshit," Gerard replied. He placed his hand on the door, right in front of Sarah's face. The muscular arm a barricade ambushing her personal space. "You know, Sarah."

Uncomfortable, Sarah took a step back, avoiding eye contact. *Not that anyone cares*, she thought. She scanned the hallway, all the other offices. By now used to the subtle alienation that arrives anytime you're not from Perry and one of three female employees at the department. The only woman of color to boot.

"I think you're really smart," Gerard said in a confident Southern twang. "You know your shit, and most of these cases, you knock 'em out of the park… But this one's different. We're talking murder in the first right now. We got the guy confessing. You know the son-of-a-bitch's crazy."

Sarah straightened her yellow blouse, keeping her cool poise. Her tall, lanky frame not ever backing down. "But that still doesn't mean we can't talk to him."

Gerard shrugged. "I mean shit, why even entertain it? Let's just book him and move on."

Amused, Sarah shook her head.

"We shouldn't waste our time on this asshole!" Gerard continued. "Just let it go and fry his ass."

"We can't just—"

Gerard gave the journal a dismissive wave. "We all know this is bullshit, Sarah—"

"Detective," Sarah corrected a playful snark in her tone.

Dimples appeared around Gerard's grin. "Right. Well. I don't know." He leaned in a little closer. Maybe too close. "Sometimes, I just think you overthink this stuff, you know."

"I just like to keep an open mind." Sarah held the journal up between them. Their Florida tension thick. Cryptic. *Maybe some real heat*, Sarah admitted to herself. "That's all. *Deputy*."

Ready for war, Sarah made her way down the hall, leaving Gerard behind. Sarah heading straight into this stage of small-town drama. Not that she had to walk too far to get to the interrogation room. The show.

Still smiling, Gerard couldn't help but watch her leave before playing catch up. Sarah's physique far from curvy but her strength still so alluring. Gerard wiped the sweat off his brow. "Your choice, Detective," he muttered.

*

The interrogation room wasn't much different than the rest of the building. Certainly far from cozy, the much-lauded A/C not helping much. There were no windows, nothing really except a table and a couple of metal chairs.

There was also a one-way mirror. One Sarah never saw anyone actually standing behind. No need for surveillance when you were talking to small-time crooks. No one approaching Kevin's notoriety that is.

Sarah and Gerard now sat side-by-side, Kevin across from them. The stranger still dressed in trendy fashion and big glasses, the headband intact. His face at a steady, stoic indifference.

At Sarah's side sat the journal and a running tape recorder. Keeping her focus on the suspect, Sarah moved her long fingers toward the book. Focusing on his unflinching bright eyes. That sly smirk. "I read several of them."

"You did?" Kevin remarked.

"Yeah. I just wanna know what the point was."

"I told you—"

"Is what you wrote true?"

"Of course, it is," Kevin said in that clinical tone. He pointed at the book. "Think about it. Why would I write that? I detailed *everything*."

"But for what? Why—"

"Why!?" Kevin cackled. He looked over at Gerard's soulless scowl. "I had to keep track for them. For the Retroactive."

"The people you worked for?" Sarah asked.

Hesitating, Kevin just smiled. "No. As a matter of fact, that's not the main reason, Detective." He shifted in his seat, surveying the barren room. The isolation.

"But I don't understand. Why write so much?"

Kevin faced her, the lousy lighting doing nothing to subdue his intensity. His sharp stare. "I did it for me."

"Well, what was the point of killing the Slaughters then?" Sarah said, keeping a cold demeanor.

Kevin scoffed. "The Slaughters? Are you seriously asking me—"

"Yeah!" Gerard growled, his round face red with rage. The stocky good looks gone by way of disgust. "We are."

Kevin matched his glare.

"Now, why the hell'd you kill the Slaughters?" Gerard yelled. "Why the hell'd you kill a little girl?"

Keeping her distance, Sarah watched Kevin slouch back. The man still so apathetic in the face of vicious allegations.

"You don't know," Kevin protested. "You don't know anything about them."

"Know what?" Sarah asked.

Kevin groaned. "I shouldn't even try…"

"Shouldn't try what?"

"I shouldn't tell you."

"You better, boy!" Gerard growled.

Sarah held her hand out, keeping the deputy at bay. Herself the perfect chill balance to Gerard's hardass act. "Tell us what you know, Kevin," she said. "Tell us everything."

All Kevin did was offer that handsome smirk as he looked Sarah right in the eye, not backing down. "That girl was gonna grow up to be a killer."

"Bullshit!" Gerard yelled.

"You heard me. If I'd let her get any older, she'd have started killing cats. Older than that, and she'd start killing kids."

Somehow Sarah shuddered in the dog days. *How'd he know...?*

"Like you!" Gerard's anger hurled back at the stranger.

Sarah gave Gerard a suspicious look. "Didn't she kill some cats?"

Awkward under her strict spotlight, Gerard put his hands up. "I don't know. They called us out there the Fourth of July."

"Yeah, for Christine Falling strangling cats," Kevin stated, not letting up.

Gerard glared at him. "It's none of your goddamn business what we're called out there for!"

The simultaneous curiosity and concern further latched into Sarah. Refusing to let go. "But wasn't it cause she was killing cats?" she asked Gerard.

Disgusted, Gerard sat back, avoiding eye contact with Gerard. A hometown pride showing through...A hometown defense. "We found a few dead cats buried there. That's all I'm saying."

Sarah waved toward their suspect. "But he's right—"

Gerard turned that glower toward her. "Look, that girl wasn't all there, Detective! You know that. Neither of them girls were."

Angry, Kevin leaned in closer, more persuasive than a preacher. "Yeah, because she was a fucking psycho!"

Gerard confronted him, the anger boiling over to an ominous power. "And you aren't?"

Kevin just gave him a chilling smile. Nothing that required serious energy...or emotion. "I've never killed a helpless animal, Deputy."

"But a child—"

"I never killed anyone that didn't deserve it!"

Now Gerard retreated in his chair a little. The nervous cracks appearing through his tough cop facade.

"What the hell does that mean?" Sarah asked Kevin. "Who are you?"

Kevin grinned at her. "You know *exactly* what I mean."

"What?"

"You read the journal, Detective."

Sarah hesitated, unable to dodge the man's gaze, even if she wanted to. *He's no idiot.* "I did."

Kevin's eyes ate her alive. Not to mention admired her struggles to keep that steady demeanor against his smoldering stare. Against his good looks. "Everything in there's true. Every. Single. Thing."

"And why am I supposed to believe that?"

"Exactly," Gerard chimed in.

Kevin scoffed. "How could I lie about something like that?"

"I don't know," Sarah started. She looked on into his baby blues. "I'm sure it's not easy to kill so many kids either."

Kevin slammed his fist on the table. "That's bullshit, and you know it!"

Unfazed, Sarah stood her ground. "Is it?"

"Those kids were gonna grow up to be a hell of a lot worse."

Matching his intensity, Sarah leaned over the table. "Were they, Kevin?"

Kevin glared at her. Offering no more words. No more tells.

Gerard said nothing. Not that he needed to. The constant glower and bad-cop demeanor all he needed to show for their 'star' suspect.

"I mean, come on, Kevin," Sarah said, somewhere between a taunt and reprimand. "These are kids we're talking about."

"Exactly!" Gerard grumbled.

"To you," Kevin replied in that methodical tone. "But where I come from, they're killers, Detective."

"But how?" Sarah responded as she sat back down. "How can you say that?"

"I see what they become."

"What!?" Gerard roared.

"Look," Sarah said. She motioned toward the book. "I read your journal."

Kevin looked on at her, no flinching, no vulnerability. A detached stare to match his smile.

"You say these kids," Sarah said. "They become 'serial killers.'"

Gerard scoffed.

"But John Gacy, Christine Slaughter—" Sarah continued.

"Christine Falling," Kevin corrected.

Sarah threw her hands up in frustration. "But again, Patsey and Ben were married—"

"And they later got divorced. Christine kept her mother's name. She'd go on to kill cats, then kids. Even babies!" Kevin's voice had become a rapid-fire encyclopedia. All on events that hadn't happened yet…not in 1970.

"So this Retroactive Project. That's who you say controls this."

"It's part of our government technically. One of their projects." Chill and confident, Kevin leaned back. Made sure to steal a pleased look over at Gerard's unwavering glare. "I served in the U.S. military up until 2035."

Even Sarah's seriousness cracked with a smile. "2035?"

"Yeah, I know." Kevin smirked. "I'm a long way from home."

"Not too far," Gerard growled. He stared straight into Kevin's soul. Or at least attempted to get through that lethargic shield. "The state prison ain't too far, boy. And neither is the loony bin." He leaned in closer, desperate to shake the so-called assassin to the core. "And that's where you'll be heading."

Like a robotic rebel without a cause, Kevin sat still. The smirk, the control, all of it unfazed.

Easy, tiger, Sarah joked to herself. *At least it's not just me Gerard plays these macho games with…*

"Now I don't believe for one second, this fairy tale shit," Gerard went on. "So I—"

Taking over, Sarah grabbed his arm, not intimidated in the slightest by that firm bicep. "Hey, let's just see what he's got to say." Out of the corner of her eye, she noticed Kevin watching her. *Felt* his curiosity. "It's his turn to talk." Ignoring Gerard's grumblings, Sarah let go of him and confronted their prime suspect. "Ain't that right, Kevin?"

Kevin still smiled. "You finish it yet, Detective?"

"I'm working on it." Sarah patted the journal, mocking the way a preacher cherishes the Bible. "But you write really well. I'll give you that."

"I've always liked to write. Just literature in general." Kevin nodded at the diary. "Even before I joined the project."

"Well, what's the point of the project then?" Sarah went on. Both Gerard and Kevin now watched her, both of them held captive by Sarah's fierce intelligence and inner fire. Her intense *interest* the opposite of TCPD's indifference. "How'd you get involved with the Retroactive?"

Kevin paused. Regardless of the glasses, his stare smothered Sarah. He took note of her vague masculinity, the type of facial expression used by neutral interviewers and judges alike. A beauty that didn't need makeup. Nor wanted it…especially when on the hunt.

Sarah clasped her hands together, zeroing in on the suspect. *There are too many details for there not to be more! He's gotta know something…* "I know you say they have the ability to send you through time. To different…"

"Killers," Kevin said.

"So the mission's to stop them before they get older?"

With cryptic, sneaky speed, Kevin moved in a little closer. "Exactly."

"That's total bullshit—" Gerard started.

"But why specifically then," Sarah interrupted, further ignoring Gerard. "They're still kids."

Finally, she got her first look at Kevin's inhibited sympathy. His smile vanished. A facial expression of regret not even he could evade.

"That has to take a toll on you," Sarah said. *Show him you care. Show him you're interested.* "I can't imagine… if all this is actually true, that is." Gerard's glare did not affect her. Not when she was in her detective groove.

Kevin pushed his glasses up his nose. "We have to stop them young."

"But that young?"

Kevin nodded. "See. Where I come from." He ran a hand through his damp hair. The air conditioning no match against the dog days. "We have real peace. These concepts of serial killers, psychopaths. They don't exist."

Gerard chuckled. Even Sarah had to flash him a smile.

"I'm serious," Kevin went on. He laid his hands on the table, detailing his past. "There's hardly any murders at all. Everything is…safe. There's caution and control. There are no assholes running around, shooting schools up—"

"That's not too common in 1970, either, buddy!" Gerard remarked.

Kevin's icy blue eyes fixated on Gerard. "You'd be surprised, Deputy," his voice keeping a calm conviction. "Our penchant for violence only grows." The smirk returned as he faced Sarah. "It only gets more ambitious." He held his cuffs-free hands up, exploiting the dangerous freedom. "You think in ten, twenty years, they'd dare let you interview a triple murderer without some sort of restraint?" An eerie chuckle escaped his lips.

The words simultaneously unnerved and wowed Sarah. *How's he so…persuasive? With this intelligence, time travel is his motive?* "So by 2040, all of this violence is gone?"

Kevin nodded. "Serial killers, mass murderers, we have them under control by then." He turned that smile toward the plodding tape recorder. The fat machine. "Our technology only gets better as well." He confronted Sarah and Gerard. "And it gets better *real fast.*"

"So why did you join the Marines?" asked Sarah in a sharp reply. "What's the point of armed services if everything is hunky-dory?"

In this claustrophobic inferno, Kevin cackled. "Hunky-dory! Wow, I haven't heard that one in a while."

Not joining in his joy, Sarah kept her unflinching focus on the 'assassin.' "Well, what's the point? Why'd you enlist? 2040 sounds an awful lot like Utopia to me."

"More like la-la land," Gerard added.

"It's like I told you, Detective," Kevin replied. The smile stayed, only his scary seriousness returned. "We're cautious. Everything is more efficient. We just take care of conflict before it gets worse."

Sarah couldn't shake the curiosity. "So there are no killers. Everyone just gets along."

"Exactly."

Skeptical, Sarah pointed at Kevin. "And the police, the military, the...the people like you. Y'all are just there for precaution."

Kevin nodded. "Most of us, yeah."

"What do you mean most of you?"

"Well, not me, obviously." He leaned back like the coolest kid in school, the coolest crook in Perry, Florida's precinct. "I'm a precaution *just* for you, Detective. For everyone in the past."

Thick tension rushed into the room. The cops got quiet. Even Gerard didn't say a word...

"The future's better," Kevin went on. "More peaceful, more advanced. We got to a point where we no longer needed to help ourselves." He leaned forward and pointed right at Sarah. "We needed to help you."

Sarah flashed a weak smile. Her only defense against this disturbing conversation, both in theme and in Kevin's passionate presentation. "So that's why...that's why you killed all those kids? To help us?"

"We had to."

"But it just—"

In a theatrical performance, Kevin pointed at himself. "Look at me, Detective. I couldn't have killed Mack Ray Edwards now, could I? 1929? Do I look sixty to you?"

Sarah tapped on the journal with a prosecutor's touch. A suspicious, compulsive rhythm. "Okay, so maybe not him. But these other cases we're looking into."

Gerard sneered. "And we're gonna get you for them."

Keeping his charismatic coolness, Kevin waved them off. "Hey, whatever you want to believe." He slumped back, savoring this spotlight. "But with all our technology, our government just wanted to help. That's why they launched the Retroactive in the first place." Sensing Sarah's intrigue, he confronted her captive curiosity. Sensing that sharp mind working overtime. "You seem to be entertaining it, Detective."

At first, startled by the sudden statement, Sarah quickly downplayed Kevin's remarks. She forced that stoic demeanor again. That brick call. *Duty calls.* "Not entertaining, but your story's...detailed." She flashed a smile. "I just can't figure out why you're doing all this."

Kevin smirked. "Come on, Detective." He leaned in a little over the table, simultaneously toying and flirting with her. "You don't believe there's the slightest chance I'm telling you the truth?"

Sarah stared him down. Her stone face a shield for the sparks. One she'd spent years perfecting for the most handsome suspects. The ones like Kevin. *Don't give him anything.*

"You read the description of Mack Ray Edwards's killer, didn't you?" Kevin teased. No one could stop him when he was on the offense. Not Sarah's detached facade nor Gerard's boiling rage.

He can have his control, Sarah thought. *For now.*

"How his mommy and daddy described the 'killer,'" Kevin continued.

Giving in, Sarah nodded. "I did."

Kevin relished the moment as he leaned back and pointed at his hair. "He had long blonde hair..." Playful, he pointed at his face. "The glasses."

Sarah held up her hand, stopping him. "Okay, so there was a resemblance."

With a triumphant laugh, Kevin threw his arms up. "And yet you still don't wanna admit it! I traveled back in time to kill him, Detective! Deal with it!"

Now Sarah fought back. She shook her head. Her steady gaze deadly. "You're convincing, Kevin, but we can't just believe science fiction stories! We need more—"

"Jesus Christ!" Gerard roared, his booming voice demanding attention. Much to Sarah's chagrin. "So now you're telling me your imaginary fantasy land wants to save little ol' us out here in Perry, Florida? That's why y'all travel across decades to kill little kids! That's a bunch of bullshit if I ever heard it!"

Sarah rolled her eyes, doing her best to match Kevin's restraint. *And this idiot's our best deputy...*

Beneath Gerard's beady glare, Kevin smirked. Amused by Sarah's reaction as well. "We have the ability." He gave a smug shrug. "So why not save innocent lives?"

"You think you're saving innocent lives!" Gerard challenged him.

Kevin's blank stare didn't panic. Instead, he started a clinical countdown on his left hand: "Samantha Evans, Matthew Nathanson, Max Hart, Tamara McConnell, David Ingram."

Intrigued, Sarah watched him in silence. *He remembers. All the names he wrote!*

Kevin held his hand out toward Gerard's face in a not-so-subtle jab, all five fingers sticking straight out for impromptu tombstones. "That's five lives we saved today, Deputy!" He glided in closer toward Gerard's gruff scowl. "And we're just talking the ones she confessed to. That ain't Patrick Myers, or God knows, all the other children she probably killed!" Then, flashing a victorious smile, he crashed back in his seat. "She even killed some babies! David Ingram was ten weeks old when that bitch suffocated him. 'Smotheration' as she called it."

Gerard turned away. "Fucking liar…"

"When'd she do this?" Sarah asked, maintaining an objective aura.

Contemplating the answer, Kevin ran his hands along his face. "Let's see… February 1980 when she killed Samantha."

"Ten years from now?"

"Right." Kevin looked right at the detective. "That little girl hasn't even been born yet."

His audience hit an uneasy quiet. The account ridiculous yet vivid. *Detailed*, Sarah thought. *Could someone this crazy act so rational and nonchalant about it? Without a camera and news crew?*

Kevin pointed over at the journal. "I got the names and dates all in there."

"Yeah, I saw," Sarah said.

"The Retroactive helps me out some." Kevin turned his bright gaze toward Sarah. "But I do most of the research."

Sarah stumbled on a response, her mind trying to unravel Kevin's fantastic tale…or at least that detective rationale was trying to. "You did all this research in the future?"

"In 2040."

Initial skepticism giving way to fascination, Sarah looked over at the journal. "There's a lot of names."

"A lot of killers."

"An awful lot of dead kids," Gerard chimed in, not bothering to disguise his ever-building disgust. A pride joining his glower once he saw Kevin face him. "Murdered ones."

"Deputy—" Sarah began.

Gerard lunged in closer. Like a schoolyard bully desperate to intimidate the stranger through strength and stature alone, only no such luck. "You're saying you're going after *every* serial killer?"

Matching Gerard's machismo, Kevin sat up straight. "We were. Yes."

Sarah kept her distance. An investigator turned investigative journalist for the moment. All eyes. All observation.

"So why do we still have these psychos running around, huh!?" Gerard yelled. With a flippant flourish, he waved Sarah toward Kevin. "The Zodiac! That asshole down in Texarkana!"

"The Phantom Killer," Kevin corrected.

Gerard glared at him. "So, why don't you kill them?" He slammed his fist on the table. His hand a man-made gavel. "Instead, you kill families! Innocent kids, you sick son-of-a-bitch!"

Silent, Sarah looked back and forth in this battle. *But how else could he get these names? All around the country.*

"Families?" Kevin scoffed. "Christine Falling's parents abused her. They molested those girls."

"Why don't you just kill yourself then?" Gerard challenged. He stared on at Kevin's blank slate. That smug apathy. "You certainly fit your own goddamn rules being a mass murderer and all!"

"I only exterminate evil, Deputy."

"Like yourself—"

"I save lives. That's my job. That's what we're all doing."

Now rattled by Kevin's continual calmness, Gerard turned to Sarah. Not surprised to see her at studious ease.

"We're only trying to help," Kevin said.

"Yeah, well," Gerard responded as he confronted the suspect. "I think you're full of shit."

"Gerard—" Sarah started.

Eager for confrontation, Gerard kept his fiery focus on Kevin. "I know you're a killer!"

The aggression always annoyed Sarah. *If he's a child killer, you really think he's gonna cave in to this…* Sarah looked over at the tape recorder, the big red light matching Gerard's angry face.

Gerard pointed toward the diary. "And you probably did kill a bunch of those kids in that sick fucking book of yours."

"Oh, I killed them, alright," Kevin remarked. His smirk beamed in this Perry, Florida dungeon. "And I saved a hell of a lot more people because of it, Deputy."

Gerard sneered. "Whatever you say, Charles Manson."

Grinning, Kevin readjusted his glasses. "I usually get Dahmer."

The agitated anger somehow increasing, Gerard's Southern fury reached new depths. "Who the hell's that?"

"I was wondering the same," Sarah said with an awkward smile.

Kevin waved them off. "Nevermind."

"But wait," Sarah said. She motioned toward Gerard. "What Gerard's saying about the Zodiac and Charles Manson's right." She looked on at their one and only suspect. "Why didn't you kill them?"

Kevin didn't flinch. He stretched for a moment. The stranger never flustered.

"If you're murdering 'serial killers' and all," Sarah went on.

Deliberating on his answer, Kevin glanced over at the recorder. "There's a lot of factors that go into that."

"Factors!?" Gerard growled.

Kevin only offered him a smile. "Well, with Manson, no one's entirely sure of his *complete* culpability."

Gerard sneered once more.

"It takes more than that to warrant an assassination. The same with all those other guys—" Kevin looked over at Sarah's ever-watchful gaze. "Or girls who were never caught."

"Like the Zodiac," Sarah commented.

"Yes." Kevin's grin only grew more mischievous. "He or she was never caught, so there's not much for us at Retroactive to do."

Still aggravated, Gerard rubbed his temple, the glower going nowhere. "That figures..."

"Those sort of unsolved mysteries, we can't help on those." Kevin waved toward the two cops. "That falls on you. *Your* era."

Now Sarah smirked. "So now you're blaming us?"

"I wouldn't say that." Kevin slumped back. "You do what you can." His eyes drifted over toward the recorder, still an amusing sight to him.

It's like he's never seen one before, Sarah thought.

"But in these times," Kevin said. "The seventies." He faced Sarah, sympathetic. "It's tough to catch them. We totally get that."

Struggling even to pretend to contemplate the confession, Gerard confronted Kevin, no hint of intrigue on that hardened face. "You just get the ones y'all know are killers? Is that it?"

Taking his time, Kevin nodded. "Yes." His smirk on Gerard stayed put. "So no, I'm not gonna track down O.J."

Sarah gave him a weird look. "O.J. Simpson?"

"There's not enough proof regardless of what—"

"Wait, you're talking about the running back!?"

"From USC," Gerard chimed in.

"That's the guy," Kevin responded.

Sarah chuckled. "He's *fineee*. You're telling me he ends up doing something?"

Tired of the questioning, Kevin threw his hands up, slight irritation crashing his arrogance. "Look, we don't know for sure! It's too much to really be certain."

Sarah was still enraptured in the entertainment. *He's acting like he's told this shit a hundred times. No way he's an actor.*

"They said the same thing about Robert Blake," Kevin went on.

"What!?" Sarah smiled. "The actor? *In Cold Blood?*"

"Yeah, and then there's Phil Spector."

"The producer?"

"He was on the girl groups?" Gerard asked.

Matching Sarah's rapid amusement, Kevin just held his hands up. Practically bored with the topic. "Look, there's no *definitive* proof either way's, all I'm saying."

"Okay, so—"

"Trust me, at this rate you'll ask me about the same people all the time."

Frustration joining the irritation, Gerard slapped his hand down, almost breaking it. Forceful enough to bring order in 'his' interrogation room. "But what about—"

"Adolph Hitler," Kevin finished, further pissing off the deputy.

"Yeah."

"It's definitely not the unknown with him."

"Exactly. So why didn't you kill his ass?"

Kevin folded his arms, keeping his cool. "Hey, look, none of you get the system."

"And what's that?" Sarah asked, pressing for more info with subtle propulsion.

Like a writer disclosing amazing secrets, Kevin placed his arms on the table, deep in thought on an answer he likely already had ready. "With a guy like Hitler, the effect is too…it's too *strong*."

"What?" Sarah asked, some disgust infiltrating her stoic armor. "What do you mean?"

"The butterfly effect."

Both Sarah and Gerard entered a quiet reflection, letting Kevin have his stage.

"Someone like Hitler's too evil. And he just affected so many lives." Kevin looked straight down, surrendering the spotlight, avoiding the cops' compelled curiosity. "We just can't risk how much it'd change." He looked at Sarah. "How much it'd change the world."

Sarah nodded, some sympathy shining through. "It's the same with Stalin?"

"All the dictators." Kevin ran a hand through his flowing hair, desperate to dodge any added stress, the horrific heat. "Barbarians, all those kinds of figures."

Ever observant, Sarah focused on Kevin's restless mannerisms. The cracks through the confidence. His constant movement and rocking. The glowing eyes behind the glasses. *He's really into this. It's his passion. His life.*

"They all just change things too much," Kevin said. He shook his head in defeat. A defeat he hated. "We can't mess with that sort of impact."

"Well, that's mighty convenient!" Gerard growled. His glare so proud. "Sounds like you can only kill certain kids."

Sarah pushed her bangs aside. "I will say that's a lot of loopholes."

"We've got no choice," Kevin said.

"I bet," Gerard commented.

Kevin placed his hands on the table. Putting himself front and center. "I told you everything." He glanced at the diary, drawing Sarah's gaze in the process. "I know you've researched what you can." He flashed a calculating smile at her. "I know you have, Detective?"

Why not play along? Sarah figured. *Just don't give him the upper hand. Only the attention.* "I've checked into a few of them, yeah."

"You connect them to me yet?" Kevin teased.

Not surrendering to his charm, Sarah offered no smile. No emotion. "There are a few similarities." She straightened her blouse. "The descriptions line up with you, of course." She locked eyes with the stranger. "But the decades are too far apart. It just doesn't add up."

"Obviously," Gerard added. His glower remained on Kevin.

Only their suspect stayed unbothered. Stayed confident. He stretched his arms across the table. His face a portrait of All-American coolness. A perfect snapshot of summer 1970…if he was even of this era. "I think you both know the truth." He flashed that megawatt smile at Sarah, unable to *visibly* get under her skin. "Even if you don't want to, Detective."

Now he's trying wayyy too hard, Sarah thought. "Who said I believed you?"

"Why wouldn't you?"

"Shit, you got no one convinced, buddy!" Gerard said. "You shoulda got a lawyer first."

Kevin's smirk persevered. His persistence perfunctory but precise. "Well, you *should* believe me." He confronted Gerard. "Where's your sheriff at anyway? Is he still out of town?"

Sarah stole a nervous look at the deputy. Gerard's glare now replaced by an unease he couldn't hide. *How the hell'd he know that?*

Flexing for a camera that wasn't there, Kevin nodded at the tape recorder. "He's missing out on this 'interview of the century.'"

"Yeah, well," Sarah said, marching through the unease. "It is Labor Day weekend." She smiled at Kevin. "But I'm guessing you picked today for that reason."

Kevin chuckled.

"This hot day in Florida," Sarah said.

"Yeah," Kevin teased. He laid his palms on the table. "He picked one hell of a time to leave town, didn't he?"

"Indeed."

"That makes it premeditated in my book," Gerard stated, the tone colder than the glare. Obviously colder than the pitiful A/C.

Not jumping in, Sarah locked in on Kevin. His otherworldly calm. *He ain't worried at all.*

"There's definitely planning involved," Kevin told the deputy. He shrugged. "After all, how do I keep getting away with it?"

"You son-of-a-bitch!" Gerard hurled at him.

"Oh, easy, Deputy!" Kevin tapped the table in a jovial rhythm. "There's a method to all this, you know."

"What fucking method? To kill a bunch of children!?"

"No." Kevin lurched forward, his movements swift and silent. His sneaky muscles grabbing Sarah's gaze...

He even moves like a killer, she thought.

"To take out the world's worst serial killers, I have to be prepared." Like a scholar, Kevin kept talking with his hands, delivering every detail. "They can't just be stray killers, mass murderers. Even your *awful, evil* dictators. There's a balance we have where I'm from. I do my damndest to avoid being seen, avoid the attention! If I do it too much, it can destroy everything."

"But what about today?" Sarah asked. "Or with the Edwards kid?"

"And I almost fucked that up." With a subdued smirk, Kevin stole a glance at the journal. "I made the history books for Mack Ray Edwards." Then he faced Sarah once more. "And I'll probably make the history books today."

Sarah nodded, struggling to hide the smile. "Probably."

"But those mistakes," Kevin went on. Channeling a Shakespearean actor, he looked backand forth between Sarah and Gerard, his Perry audience. "They happen, but it can't be too often. The Project doesn't like that. You see, we can't change history too much. But we can do what we can to get shit done."

Sarah was getting swayed. Not by the story but Kevin's steadfast beliefs. *Maybe there's truth somewhere in the science fiction. Somewhere...*

In a final gesture, Kevin pointed a few fingers at Gerard's disapproval. His permanent glare. "We're only trying to help you."

Expecting her partner's impending meltdown, Sarah waited a second. From her perspective, Kevin seemed to too. *Almost like he's hoping for confrontation. Enough to get under Gerard's skin. Find his tell. His breaking point.*

But it never came. Gerard's silence was his only response. His skeptical, disgusted silence.

Kevin turned to Sarah. "I know this all sounds crazy, Detective, but you just have to trust me. I didn't come here to lie. Especially to you." He flashed a sly smile at Gerard. "I'm here to help."

Gerard's temper didn't respond. Not yet.

"I don't know," Sarah said. She slumped back in her seat, somewhat letting her guard down to reveal a sympathetic soul to the one and only suspect. *Level with him*, she reminded herself. *Make him at ease.* Concepts Gerard and his Perry ilk would never grasp. "I just think there are better methods."

"Better methods?" Kevin replied, his voice dismissive and distant.

He sounds stunned. "Well, yeah," Sarah went on. "If we're all in Utopia like you say."

"It's very peaceful."

"And I get that. So then." Stumbling on her overwhelming thoughts, Sarah pushed her bangs aside once more. "Why kill them? Especially when they're children."

Kevin just grinned. "I already explained—"

"Not really." Before Kevin could respond, Sarah slid the journal in front of her, taking command. "Instead of murder and with y'all's technology and progress, why can't you rehabilitate them?"

Scoffing, Kevin tilted his head back. An arrogant amusement shining through. "Rehabilitate serial killers?"

"Yeah."

"Well, I see how that's worked for you." Still grinning, Kevin waved around the room. "This place is a fucking dump! These penitentiaries are a joke!"

"They should be a dump!" Gerard added with anger.

"But we're not 2040," Sarah said to the stranger. "If you're telling us the truth, and we as a society have made that much progress, why not, I don't know, kidnap the children and bring them to the future?"

Turning away, Kevin avoided her questions. Her persuasion.

"You don't have to kill them, Kevin," Sarah said. "You can give them another chance. Try to change them."

Kevin smirked at her. The chilling confidence now rushing back. "Who says we don't?"

"Well—"

"Four-hundred thousand children go missing in the States every year, Detective." Kevin's blue eyes fixated on her. As did his entire focus. "You don't think some of those came with me?"

Not backing down, Sarah held on to the diary, suppressing any nerves. *It's all part of his game. His show*, she reminded herself. "You never mentioned that part of the Retroactive."

Kevin's sly chuckle echoed through the hollow room. Such a lonely noise. "Well, in all honesty, we've learned you can't cure pure evil." He ran a hand along his toned arm. "There's too much risk in letting them live."

"But still," Sarah said. "Children?"

The smile disappeared. Kevin's mood shifted to a serious rumination. A haunted state of mind he couldn't forever hide. "They start young. You've got no idea, really." He scoffed as he readjusted the headband. "At this point, you've got nothing that even studies serial killers, do you? Not in 1970?"

Not answering, Sarah looked down at the diary. She, Gerard, and 1970 American law enforcement put on the spot.

"You know nothing about them or their evil," Kevin went on, fear hitting his chill vibes for once. "Just how dangerous they are!" He leaned in closer, commanding the cops' attention. Their shared unease. "Most of them start young, killing animals, building that...*hunger*. Hell, some of them kill people before they're even teenagers!"

Neither Sarah nor Gerard said anything. They couldn't in the face of the eerie information. The sheer shock.

"We try to get them before they go too far," Kevin said. The audience at his mercy, he shook his head, weariness weighing him down. The sympathetic sadness he didn't like to show. "I try to exterminate them before they even hurt animals, to be honest."

Sarah nodded, offering support while goading him on. "I can't blame you there," she reassured. *Keep him talking. He's lying, but maybe the truth'll come out...his version at least.*

"There's too much risk in them," Kevin said. "Maybe they're born that way, or maybe they're molded through tragedy and shit parents. I don't know." He pointed at the journal. Gone from lethargic assassin to amateur psychoanalyst. Embattled bitterness starting to escape. "All I know's we can't cure those psychos. Their *inherent* evil." Leaning back, he shook his head slowly. "Not even in 2040."

"So you're saying you have no choice but to kill them?"

"They put everyone at risk. The entire world!" Holding Sarah hostage to his analytical eloquence and mannerisms, Kevin leaned forward. "We *have* to kill them and kill them young, Detective!"

The morbid moment lingered. There in a room full of humidity and dread. All bloodlust, sweat, and fears.

Sarah hesitated in the silence. Now she could even *sense* Gerard's discomfort. *Now he's got the big bad deputy scared.* "But there's just," Sarah started. She opened up the journal, the page *crinkling* like a centuries-old text. On to a random page full of scribbled names and locations. Not that the other pages were much different. Kevin's handwriting always meticulous and clean. "There are just so many names." She flipped through the pages, revealing endless entries. "Are there really that many serial killers, Kevin?"

Unable to help himself, Gerard leaned over, getting a front-row seat to the systematic hit list. To this written crypt.

Out of the corner of her eye, Sarah saw fright overtake Gerard's Southern toughness. Saw him run a hand through his short hair. She couldn't help but smile. That is until Kevin responded.

"More than you'll ever know," the suspect said, his tone hushed and filled to the brim with a suppressed torment. A suppressed fear.

Sarah looked right at those blue eyes. Now it was Kevin's turn to look away, hiding in his diary. *Why's he squirming now?* she wondered.

"There are even some I'd never heard of," Kevin went on. "Killers I didn't even know existed," he said as his voice cracked. A slight shiver shot through his snarky confidence. "Ones that were never caught. They just kept killing. Killing everybody…"

Before Sarah's stern gaze, Kevin now rocked back andb forth. His face a crumbling brick wall. His silence speaking volumes to this detective. *He believes it enough. So much so the revenge fantasy traumatized him.*

"You alright?" Gerard barked at him.

Overtaking Gerard, Sarah closed the journal. "Kevin."

Kevin kept rocking in his seat, for once, avoiding his audience.

Sarah reached toward him. Obviously keeping her distance. "Listen, Kevin. We'll look into these names—"

In a sudden motion, Kevin reached over and *MASHED* stop on the tape recorder. The mechanical pop echoed through the room.

Kevin's quick movement made Gerard jump back.

"Shit!" the deputy shouted.

But Sarah stayed put. Inches away from the man believed to have killed a seven-year-old girl.

They locked eyes. Kevin's calmness the opposite of her anxious anticipation. He was no longer at war with himself...At least for now.

"I need coffee," said his dry tone.

Keep him comfortable, Sarah thought. *Keep him open.* "Okay," she said. "We can take a break."

"Jesus Christ!" Gerard groaned. "You wanna give him a cigarette break too?"

"Why not?" Kevin replied instantly. His apathetic expression drew Gerard's glare. Not to mention Sarah's continual intrigue. "It's not like you don't do it all the time for the other suspects."

Amused by the stranger's sense of humor, Sarah enjoyed Gerard's steady grumbles. His silent, repressed rage while on the clock. *Kevin likes this shit. But how far does the madness go?*

"But I'm fine," Kevin told them. He stole a smirk at Gerard. "Smoking kills, you know."

"Does it really?" a curious Sarah asked.

Kevin faced her. "Trust me. We know where I come from."

Chapter 5

Hot. That's how Guanajuato, Mexico felt in the heart of summer. The uncomfortable humidity still haunts me...still draws a sweat from my subconscious.

The white tanktop, the highwater volley shorts offered me no solace from this sweltering landscape. Then again, being out on poverty row, out by the array of Mexico's most dilapidated shacks, didn't offer me much shade. There were no trees, much less A/C. But still, I kept journeying along the battered sidewalk and intermittent patches of dirt. Through this field of ugly Ford pickups and even uglier mailboxes.

Distant mariachi music dominated the scene. The soothing songs echoing off phonographs from practically every household.

But not many people were around. The locals forced inside on such a hideous, humid day. Plus, by now, I was a few hundred miles from Mexico City. Far from any sense of civilization.

All the while, I kept the Browning pistol tucked in my waistband. Ready for my reach. But for now, I just needed to get to my target: Delfina de Jesus Gonzalez.

She was there in her front yard as I expected. Living in abject poverty. The parents who neglected her nowhere in sight. I had the girl all to myself…except for the child sitting next to her, Delfina's younger sister Maria.

The girls were somewhat similar, but Maria looked to have inherited a prettier face compared to Delfina's rugged canvas even in such youth. Delfina was short and stout, her build like that of a Pit Bull ready to strike at any second. On the other hand, her sister was still innocent. Still scrawny and jubilant.

Beneath the blistering sunshine, I could see the two dark-haired girls playing with an array of baby dolls. Some of the toys half-naked, some dismembered. Quite appropriate considering the life Delfina would go on to live.

I stopped a few feet away, the adrenaline eating at my core. Not to mention the unease. Delfina was only sixteen but looked years younger. Still, I knew the dark truth. I knew she'd go on to run a Bordello From Hell that'd kill over ninety people.

There she and her sister were playing in the dirt. No grass or flowers allowed on such barren soil. Nothing pretty. This was a low-class desert. One in which the imagination was the only escape for the neighborhood's children.

Preparing myself for the attack, I wiped sweat off my head. Pushed back my short blonde hair and readjusted those glasses. But there wasn't much convincing to do. Not when I was assigned to kill someone so evil.

The time was now. I withdrew the gun and ambushed their playtime.

No caring parents and no nosy neighbors meant Delfina didn't have a chance. Her shrill Spanish unable to sway me. I never could speak the language that well.

I fired a bullet in her greasy face.

The shot sprayed blood all over the dolls. Over her screaming sister.

The teenager's body then collapsed into the dirt. Delfina's blood forming a red fountain pouring from her mouth, from the brutal bullethole.

I didn't have time to hesitate. I turned toward Maria. The three-year-old I knew would grow up to be a monster aiding and abetting in Delfina's sickening spree.

I pointed the pistol at her.

Behind a forced glower, I contemplated her crimes. Her future torment. A futile attempt at coercing a merciless stance.

Maria's sobs overpowered the deafening mariachi marathon. Her weeping hitting deep into my heart. There in the heat, I got a chill just watching such pitiful sadness. Her helplessness…hearing that high-pitched Spanish accent…watching a child covered in her sister's hand-me-downs and splattered flesh…

There was no choice. No other option. I closed my eyes and pulled the trigger.

Chapter 6

August 23, 2015

I didn't know *exactly* where to go. Or what time I should be there. All I knew was I had to kill David Wash for this mission.

Around 2033, Wash began his killing spree in and around Atlanta, Georgia. The thirty-year-old that sickening combination of child killer and pedophile. The disturbing archetype amongst the lowest scum humanity had to offer. He wasn't caught 'til after the sixth little girl went missing…after he'd slit her throat before police could get him. None of his victims over the age of ten.

The Georgia Boogeyman was finally imprisoned a year before I got the honorable discharge. Just a few years before the Retroactive hired me. Wash one of the world's last famous serial killers…until we stepped in.

Now I was about to wipe his record clean and save six girls in the process.

Deep down, I was excited. I had the chance to go home for the first time since I had enlisted. I'd been avoiding Stanwyck, Georgia for over a decade. But now, I at least had an excuse to exorcise these demons. A chance to distance myself from the same middle school Wash and I attended back in 2015.

I stumbled through the south Georgia heat. Past the empty sprawling brick tombstone buildings comprising Stanwyck Middle

School (a school for the seventh and eighth graders). At five o'clock, the administration and teachers were long gone. Had long made their desperate escape from this Title 1 Hell. The students and parents long abandoning this public prison as well…most of them at least.

Like the seventh grade reunion I never wanted, I walked through this all-too-familiar ghost town. As alone and alienated as I was at twelve years old. No support, no friends. Much less a girlfriend.

Around me, there were no cars in sight. The surrounding middle-class neighborhood with no sign of life. From my own experiences, I knew the cameras at this shithole didn't work. Never mind the security guards that left their shift early.

I knew I had plenty of time.

Making my way along the battered parking lot, I straightened my glasses. The fohawk letting my blonde bangs not bother me for once. The tight jeans and tucked-in red button-down shirt allowed me to pass off as an aloof teacher if push came to shove. Or if anyone around here actually gave a shit.

I stepped onto the desolate track field. No one was practicing, no one driving down the narrow street behind it. No students were out and about, nowhere except the spot that compelled me.

See, this August day brought anguish. For once, the Friday afternoon had dread instead of joy…especially since I knew what horror was in store. What I had to do.

I wasn't *positive* where Retroactive wanted me to go, but I had a gut feeling. A preteen memory. A quick flash from my most disturbing interaction with The Georgia Boogeyman.

During the long walk beneath a blistering sun, I ignored the sweat and anxious adrenaline. After all these 'kills,' I still wasn't used to it, man. Then again, who would be? Especially when you were assigned to assassinate a childhood classmate.

My gaze stayed on the few oak trees toward the back. The few shady spots this scene had to offer in the summertime. And also one of the few spots where troublemakers could seek shelter from the superintendents. David Wash amongst them.

I saw him from afar. Shrouded on the outskirts of this Stanwyck schoolyard. By the chain-link fence, beneath the tall trees in his own desolate, demented world.

I knew he wouldn't see me. David was an idiot to put it mildly. I never had any academic classes with the guy, but when you were a loser like me, well, you talked to who you could at gym and lunch. Any way to avoid being alone and bullied. I suppose listening to David's compulsive lies about which hot girl he'd fucked or sexted was better than getting called ugly or whatever other gay slur was trending for the day.

Even then, I knew how David was. I'd seen him display his sick tendencies even at that age. And today was no different.

Relying on memory, I strolled past the stray pavement, the cluttered weeds, and the rusting metal bleachers. The closer to my target I got, the more I heard high-pitched arguing from male and female voices. Their middle school voices still developing.

Now everything came rushing back. I didn't need to check the iPhone 6 to know where I was. The senses set in. The horrible humidity. The silence of a seventh grade Friday afternoon. all while the nerves returned. I knew *exactly* what day this was. And I dreaded facing it again. Even with twenty-five years extra experience and that PMR-30 pistol hidden in my back pocket.

A sudden *SLAP* made me run faster. Then came that painful scream.

I came to a stop at my final destination. The oaks blocked the blinding sunlight, giving me a crystal clear view of the scene before me. Whatever faint comforting coolness there was instantly overtaken by the chills creeping through my body.

There lurked The Georgia Boogeyman as I remembered him. Not as the bearded, six-foot slob who slaughtered six little girls but the shorter, ADD-riddled middle schooler with a buzz cut. Dressed in wrinkled jean shorts and a UGA Bulldogs tee, David stood up over the first victim of his perverse pleasure: Michelle Beckley.

On the ground, our classmate cowered against a tree. Blood trickled down her pale face. Her bright eyes aghast at David's emotionless glare. Her long red hair now ravaged with dirt and scattered leaves. The girl was slow, but that was no excuse for David's disgusting plans. Now here she was, helpless. Too frightened to even notice me standing a few feet away...

David was too enthralled in his evil to notice me either.

The surreal scene paralyzed me for a moment. I was back in my youth. A morbid memory I yearned to forget. Now the empathy sunk into me once more. Not for the killer I needed to dispatch…but for his victim.

The girl was weeping, unable to say anything. Michelle was at this fucking sicko's mercy. This time, I didn't need to wait. I knew exactly what David would do to her. How he'd rape her right beneath that oak. Right here at our hated middle school.

David made his move. Lunging forward, he pulled Michelle's purple Stanwyck Middle tee shirt down, revealing her bra. Her tight shorts the rapist's next target.

She cringed at his crude touch. The tears intensifying.

Fighting my own trembling emotions, I withdrew the PMR-30 and pointed it right at the fucker. Ready to exterminate his decades of death and suffering right there. "David Wash!" I yelled.

David stood up and glared at me. Outside of the flabby belly, he looked like an innocent seventh grader rather than a future serial killer. But of course, I knew better. I'd known the vile son-of-a-bitch since grade school.

My glare intensified. Ignoring Michelle's scared confusion, I held on to the gun. Ready to release this bitter, painful memory…

"Who the fuck are you?" said David's obviously frightened Southern squeal.

Then I saw David's expression go from fear to intrigue.

No surprise. I gave a quick turn, just enough to see me: the nerdy twelve-year-old boy walking across the track field. A narrow cardboard box in hand. The scrawny kid wearing those huge glasses literally following in my footsteps.

Back in 2015, I'd come across David and Michelle. I met where he told me to. But the plan was to trade baseball cards, not rape a classmate. Needless to say, I didn't participate.

I confronted David's slowly-forming smile. His perverse confidence.

Before kid-me could get any closer and before David could get any more hope, I raised the pistol and fired a warning shot.

I knew myself better than anyone. Back then, I was a total chickenshit.

And I was right. One glance back showed twelve-year-old Kevin hauling ass the other way. Back to his childhood home right across the street. I'd done the same so many years ago…but now I was gonna make things right. I trusted my parents *too* much back then. Trusted *this fucking town* too much.

I kept my eerie cool. I wasn't pressed for time. I set my sights back on David and his victim. On David's dejected glower.

I waved the gun at Michelle. "Run! Go home!"

At my plea, Michelle hauled ass. Off to where kid-me disappeared.

Alone with the killer himself, I aimed at David. Felt a slight breeze whip against these dress-code-approved clothes. But I stood strong. This time, I wouldn't run away and leave a young girl to be molested. I wouldn't trust disapproving adults anymore. Not when *I* was the adult now.

My unblinking eyes met David's scowl. And so did the gun.

"What the hell are you gonna do!?" David's high-pitched tone yelled. Sounding tough impossible with such a voice. "I didn't do anything!"

I just kept pointing the PMR-30 at the inevitable pedo. No need for a more quiet gun when there'd be no one around the school. The execution.

Nervous, David held his hands up. "I didn't do anything. I swear!"

For the first time on the job, I felt no reservations. No hesitation on that kill shot. No flinching when the young flesh and grue splattered over me. This was redemption.

Chapter 7

Even in May, England was cold. Especially today.

The wind whipped against my long blonde hair as I followed the eleven-year-old girl. Followed her inside the abandoned house in the heart of these dreary slums. The blue-collar neighborhood a graveyard of broken dreams and families.

1968 was a brutal year. A violent year. My current assignment the latest addition to its growing body count.

But at the moment, the guilt returned. The eternal existential crisis. All those young eyes stayed with me. The kids' innocence in the face of a loaded gun haunting me like never-ending shock therapy to my senses.

After all, removed from adulthood and their notorious crimes, these were just children. Most of them abused, molested, impoverished. Most of them victims before the evil ever took hold.

I just had to remind myself what they'd become if I didn't stop them. I was saving these doomed souls after all, giving them an early funeral rather than waiting on that inevitable execution. Because of me, they could be mourned as children instead of monsters. And in the afterlife, they'd now have a clean record for whatever was waiting for us all.

Dressed in tight bell-bottoms and a green Army jacket, I fit right in here in 1968. I wore a red bandana. The outfit complete with the Colt Cobra .38 special I kept hidden in my coat pocket. Perfect for the era.

Through the desolation, I marched on toward that two-story yellow house, past the foreclosed stores. No one else was in sight. No children, no bums.

I made my way inside that drafty old house.

The shattered windows offered no solace from the cold. Neither did the busted-down front door.

Surrounding me were barren walls. There was no electricity, no lighting. I readjusted my glasses in this noon darkness.

The house felt empty, void of all life. Hell, there wasn't even a cigarette or beer bottle. Not even the homeless wanted a part of this place.

My feet carried me down the hall. I heard nothing but silence save for the creaking, groaning floorboard. And my own pounding heart.

Nervous, I reached inside my pocket. Felt the soothing touch of the pistol.

Still, I wasn't sure where the girl was. Maybe the target hadn't seen me. Maybe she wasn't even here.

Then I entered the long living room. The fireplace was coated by centuries of ashes. The walls were bland, the windows offering weak lighting in this abandoned arena.

I thought I was alone…until I saw a boy lying in the corner. A tiny four-year-old child. Unconscious and helpless. Duct tape tied his wrists. Covered his small mouth. Specks of red stained his golden hair.

The child laid there as if he were on a silver platter. Awaiting the sadistic touch of whoever did this to him. Whoever wanted to kill him.

Chills overtook me. My body went hollow in horror.

Then a wild cry erupted behind me.

Frightened, I whirled around.

That's when I got my first close look at The Tyneside Strangler: Mary Bell. An eleven-year-old from Hell.

She lunged at me, knocking me to the ground.

Mary's narrow eyes focused on me. Her black bob-cut accentuated a round face, the permanent scowl. Beneath the gray blouse was the body of a young killer, one with strength beyond her years.

Snarling, Mary fastened those fat hands around my throat. The compulsion compelled her. The need to strangle and kill. A disgusting desire that'd been devouring her these past few months.

Struggling in her death grip, I cried out. I struggled to breathe. Felt my face go red. Mary's depraved cravings only made her stronger.

Simultaneous adrenaline and excitement hit the girl's face. I didn't see innocence. Just a most wicked pleasure.

I looked over at the boy. He was still out. Still helpless. Ready to be Mary's unfortunate first victim. After she was done with me, that is.

My hands fumbled for my coat pocket. Desperately searching for the gun. The executioner's blade just at my fingertips.

"Die!" Mary screamed in a voice colder than this house. Colder than the abusive mother and father she had back "home." Colder than the empty soul buried beneath her body.

Like a wild animal, she leaned in closer. Eager to finish the kill. Ready to start her killing spree with this thirty-five-year-old man.

I stared at Mary's smirk and sadism. Rather than the usual empathy, I felt rage. Disgust. No remorse at all for exterminating this evil one. No reluctance. Mary Bell was a monster. Even as a child.

Finally, I grabbed the pistol. Put it to her chilling smile. Pulled the trigger.

Chapter 8

In her messy office, Sarah was alone with a killer. Or alone with his words, at least. The journal a portal away from Perry, Florida and into the heart of this mystery.

The door was open, but it didn't matter. The hallway lights long off. Most of the TCPD cops and detectives done for the night. Their indifference clear even with the city's biggest murder case in decades right at their fingertips. Her co-workers didn't have Sarah's drive or passion. That much was obvious to anyone observant like her. Especially given how desperate the department was to name her Lead Detective.

Regardless of what was turning into a graveyard shift, there was Sarah still at her desk, immersed not in the cup of coffee but that journal. The writings of Kevin the Assassin. These latest entries leaving Sarah stunned but fascinated.

Sarah looked up from the Mary Bell account. Recovering from Kevin's pristine prose. *Why would he write so much? Who'd be this dedicated?*

Sarah thumbed through the rest of the diary. There wasn't much left.

THUNDER blared outside. Startled, Sarah turned and looked out the room's only window.

Nightfall was upon Perry. The downtown district pitch black other than the occasional streetlight. The occasional lightning flash in the sky's ominous backdrop.

Sarah took another sip. The caffeine a much-needed break from the unease building inside. This most bizarre mystery consuming her curiosity.

He's one hell of a storyteller, she thought. Sarah's eyes drifted down to the crisp pages. *Maybe this really is one of those unexplained mysteries. That Twilight Zone shit.*

She turned to see Brandon looking right at her. The handsome son. Rosehead Park at its prettiest all because of him. Now Sarah's heart interrupted her focus. Her detective's spirit. But not for long.

Again, thunder erupted, but Sarah didn't flinch this time. Instead, she got to work and put the coffee down. Continuing her isolated investigation.

Immersed, Sarah snatched a small notepad. On the first page were several names she'd scribbled down throughout this journey...all of Kevin's victims, both real or imagined. His serial killer list.

Sarah grabbed a pen. "Are you really 'exterminating evil,' weirdo?" She jotted down a new name: *Mary Bell.*

Lightning flashed across Sarah's face. Leaning back, she pushed her sweaty bangs to the side. Not bothered by the storm, much less the soft raindrops. Not bothered by anything except her hunt for the truth. *Why would he go through all this? Why write all this shit down?*

A quick *KNOCK* disrupted Sarah's brainstorm. She turned to see Gerard standing there, his height allowing him to grip the top of the doorway, highlighting his biceps, not that Sarah minded.

Smiling, Gerard pointed down the hall. "Hey, Paul's done looking up those names you were asking about."

"Okay," Sarah replied.

"He got that miniature phone thing too. Or whatever the hell that is."

Sarah chuckled. "Alright, I'm ready."

Gerard pointed toward the clock. "He's just bitchin' we kept him waitin'."

Smirking, Sarah stole a glance at the time. *7:30.* "It's not even that late."

"Around here it is." Then, with a flirtatious smirk, Gerard stepped out into the hallway.

Sarah couldn't help but steal an admiring look at Gerard's bubbly ass. His muscular physique so striking even in the darkness was literally popping in that uniform.

As if he sensed Sarah's smoldering stare, Gerard flashed that smile at her once more. Dimples and all. This police department not the place Sarah ever expected to be checking out hot twenty-four-year-olds.

Really, girl? she scolded herself. Doing her best to play off getting caught, she quickly closed the journal and grabbed the notepad.

Gerard leaned in toward the office. "You coming?" his Southern accent teased.

Battling the heat both inside and out, Sarah staggered to her feet. "Yeah, hold on."

*

The two of them were back in the war room, back to the interview with a suspected child killer. Not that much had changed. Kevin stayed cool and collected in his same seat. Gerard and Sarah right across from him, the tape recorder recording this next round.

Clinging to a half-empty cup of coffee, Kevin surveyed the room. The one-way mirror no one would be lurking behind this late. Not at a defunct department like Perry's.

To Sarah, the lights seemed dimmer. Regardless of the steady rain, an uneasy hush overtook the room. The humidity and claustrophobia not going anywhere. The loneliness of the late shift.

But Sarah had come too far now. Detective Barlow needed answers and explanations. She was the only perfectionist in this precinct. The only one with passion. And besides, if things went too awry, there was always that rookie deputy sleeping in the lobby for back-up.

Just keep him talking, Sarah reminded herself. With both Gerard's dutiful boredom and Kevin's gleaming gaze glued to her,

Sarah placed a Ziploc bag on the table, laying Kevin's cell phone next to the journal. "We ran the names," Sarah said, keeping her tone strong. In control. "You weren't lying."

Kevin nodded.

"Not completely anyway," Sarah added.

"I'm telling the truth," Kevin said. He held up the coffee, letting steam decorate him like fog in a cemetery. "Those kids would've grown up to be serial killers. That's the only part you don't get, I'm afraid." He took a quick sip. "The only part you'll never know."

As he put the cup down, Sarah looked at Kevin, her stoic mask hiding all intrigue. "But that's the problem, Kevin. There are no criminal records for any of these kids. John Wayne Gacy, Ted Bundy, Aileen Wuornos. If you did kill them all like you said, you were killing innocent people."

Kevin shook his head. "None of them are innocent."

Gerard glared at him. "And we're just supposed to believe you."

Scoffing, Kevin waved toward the journal. "Compare what I wrote to what happened! The damn stories line up, don't they!"

Fighting back, Gerard slammed his fist on the table. The brute force causing some of Kevin's coffee to splash out. Gerard pointed at Kevin's lingering smirk. His arrogant indifference. "Watch it, boy! We're the cops around here, not you!"

"So you say," Kevin said, not even trying to suppress that sly snark. "You're the *good guys*, right?"

Sarah placed a hand on Gerard's shoulder, intervening. "Hey, it's cool," she calmed Gerard.

The deputy leaned back in his seat, all as the glower only grew more fierce.

"Look, Kevin," Sarah said. "The killings, the murder weapons, and witnesses…they all line up, sure."

"Just like I wrote," Kevin remarked in that clinical tone.

Sarah hesitated. *He's not backing down. Either he's convincing himself or maybe he's starting to convince me.* "Well. Yeah. Some of the shooters were described as looking similar to—"

"Me."

Matching Kevin's lethargic confidence, Sarah forced a smile. "Well, it's all public record."

"So?" Kevin pointed at his outfit from the hair down to the glasses. "You think I just gave myself this costume, Detective." Making sure not to aim at either cop, Kevin flashed them a finger gun. "That I Killed Christine Falling the same exact way I killed all the others." He laid his hand on the table. Outside, the loudest thunder yet coincided with his move. "Just to be a copycat killer."

Sarah and Gerard stayed silent. Their expressions that of two scientists studying a subject that both fascinated and horrified them.

"How could I even do this research?" Kevin went on. He leaned in closer, not from defensive desperation but boisterous bemusement. "Find out about so many cases spanning *decades*." Behind the glasses, he locked in on Sarah. Only she wasn't gonna squirm. Not on her watch. "It's 1970, Detective. It's not that easy. Not today anyway."

Some stress snuck into Sarah. Through the allure and dread. Not that Gerard's glare was helping. Nor was the fact this was the weirdest murder suspect she'd ever encountered. *He's trying you!* "It'd take a lot of work for sure," she said to Kevin. Sarah then sat up straight, not playing tough but not showing any sympathy toward him. Not revealing how hooked she was to his story. "But anyone can do the research." She gave him a smile. "Anyone crazy enough."

Kevin scoffed. "Come on…"

"You can't just expect us to take your word! Especially if you did kill the Slaughter family."

"I've already proven myself."

Sarah's focus stayed on Kevin, ready to further excavate his mind. Whatever soul he had left. "You say you're from the future, but you've got murders of people you wrote about that I've never heard of. That *no one's* ever heard of."

Amidst the rain and Sarah's attack, Kevin grabbed the coffee. Desperate for a momentary distraction.

Now we got him. Sarah wasn't slowing down. "Jeffrey Dahmer, David Wash. You went all the way to twenty-twenty, man."

Flashing that rare rattled expression, Kevin almost dropped the drink before slamming it back down, splashing more of its hot remnants.

"I mean listen, Kevin," Sarah's strength continued. "We can't take you seriously if you're not even gonna make sense! You need to tell us the truth. That's all we want!"

Struggling against the spotlight, Kevin chuckled. One of defeat rather than his typical arrogance. "What the hell do you think I've been doing?"

With both hands, Sarah smashed the table, again synchronizing herself to another terrifying burst of thunder. Mirroring its intensity with anger she saved for special occasions. Like now.

Gerard jumped.

Kevin's laugh died instantly.

Now Sarah had the suspect's full and undivided attention. *He's either crazy or pure evil…No different than the other losers. Now's the time to strike!* She pointed toward the door, her glare all the more intimidating and raw due to its rarity. "There's a family out there you killed in cold blood, Kevin! Now." She leaned in closer, taking command of this stage. "I've got all fucking night to figure you out. You're not getting away with anything. You're damn sure not going free, so why not make this easy on everyone and tell us why you did it?"

Kevin hesitated in the heat. But his vacant, pale expression didn't budge, not even this drenched in sweat. "I already did. It's my—"

"You're full of shit, Kevin!" Sarah said in an aggressive attack. "Just admit it. It's all lies and bullshit. You didn't travel back in time. It's all in your mind! These are cases and murders you probably saw on T.V."

"Look, to do that much research and read into all these cases," Kevin stumbled. In a flustered motion, he waved at the journal. "It'd take me weeks, months to do that right now! But in the future, man..." He shook his head in disbelief. "It takes fucking minutes." Thunder roared in from the night. "Look, none of you get it! It's too early. You just. You don't understand how many killers are out there." Frustrated, he looked off at his coffee, avoiding their piercing stares. "I guess... I guess I can't blame you. It's not the same culture right now. Not the same that we have where I come from." He grabbed the mug and shook the cold leftovers. No sugar or cream in the black debris. "You don't have the same amount of information and data." He gave the cops a weak smile. "Not for a few more years at least."

Doing her best to downplay these many details, Sarah sighed. "You're telling us a lot, man, I'll say that." *Understatement of the year*, she joked to herself. Sarah slid the phone toward him.

"But is this where you're supposed to be getting all your information from?"

Kevin gave it a glance before smirking. "Shit. You won't believe me anyway."

"Try me."

Still grinning, Kevin deliberated on an answer.

Is he really lying? Sarah couldn't help but wonder. *Is this how he came up with over twenty stories? All of it lies*? She pointed at the iPhone. "Is this from the future?"

Kevin looked at the device once more. "Yeah." He faced Sarah. "It's an iPhone."

"What the hell!?" Gerard chuckled. "An I-phone? Is that some sort of space phone or something?"

Even Sarah had to crack a smile. Amidst Gerard's howling laughter, Kevin smirked back at them.

He's not embarrassed at all. Sarah noticed how unfazed their suspect always was. The smirk more assured than anything.

"More like a computer, I guess you could say," Kevin said.

"Like on *Star Trek*?" Gerard joked. He slapped the table. "Goddamn, whatcha gonna tell us next! You got a flying saucer out by Rosehead."

Skeptically, Sarah held up the cell phone. "You mean this little thing has all that information?"

"You'd be surprised," Kevin quipped.

"Right, 'cause it's the future?" Gerard taunted.

"A lot can change in seventy years," Kevin responded, no timidity in his tone.

Sarah gazed down at the phone. Through the plastic, she made out a screen, the smaller buttons. The item a black slab of metal, a monolith less than seven inches. "Well, how do you..." Scoffing off her own compelled curiosity, she confronted the stranger. "How do you travel through time with this thing?"

Kevin nodded at it. "The Retroactive has it programmed. When it's on, I can go anywhere."

"All on this phone?" Sarah asked.

"What, do you teleport?" Gerard scoffed.

"No," Kevin said. He smiled at the deputy. "It's a little bit more than that."

Sarah laid the iPhone on the table. "So, what's the process?"

Looking on at Sarah, Kevin ran a hand through his flowing hair. "It just depends on them, I guess."

"The Retroactive?"

"Yes. Whenever they need me to leave." Kevin motioned toward the phone. "They send me through that."

"It's that easy?" Sarah asked behind a suspicious smile.

"It's more powerful than you think." No one now flinched in the storm. Everyone attuned to Kevin's scary sincerity. "You don't need much of a charge either."

"What do you mean, charge?" Gerard remarked.

The stranger's smile only grew wider. Using his hands, Kevin explained the process. "I mean, it's like a car battery. You have to keep it going." He waved the cops toward the cell. "But with this phone, that battery can last days sometimes."

"Days?" Gerard responded in disbelief.

"Well…" Kevin gave them a facetious shrug. "That's pretty damn good in the future."

Sarah grinned. "You're *very* convincing. I'll give you that." She ran her hands along her arms, keeping her cool at a skeptical distance. "But this is all very…science-fictiony."

"Really?" Kevin groaned.

"*Star Trek*," Gerard told him. "That whole, what is it..." He looked over at Sarah. "That whole beam me up shit."

Sarah caved in with a chuckle. "That's how it sounds."

Annoyed if amused, Kevin shook his head. "I figured you two wouldn't get it."

Here he goes again, Sarah realized. "It's not that-" she started.

"Like I said," Kevin interrupted. He moved in closer, holding Sarah's gaze captive. "It's just too soon for you." He clapped his hands together. The sound even startling Gerard. "You can't realize all this in 1970! I mean, I get it!" His smile teased the cops. "What I'm saying won't make sense for *decades*, Detective."

Sarah scoffed. Partly from frustration, partly from a *fear* Sarah didn't wanna acknowledge. Not necessarily due to Kevin's message or his suspected murders but his sheer conviction. *Just stay on him. Get him on the defense, Sarah.* "But I don't get it," she said, forcing a hardened monotone. Sarah pointed at the phone. "If this thing can help you escape, why not use it now?"

Having Gerard and Sarah study every move didn't bother Kevin. Instead, he took a calm breath before looking on at Sarah's intense expression. "I can't." Then, he gave them that chilling smile. "My work isn't done here, Detective."

Sarah didn't avoid his grin. Didn't avoid Kevin's cryptic arrogance. "And why's that?"

"I've got my reasons." Kevin grabbed the mug. "I can't leave just yet." Clinging to the cup, he swirled the coffee about in the mug. No interest in drinking it. The coffee just a minor diversion. "They won't let me."

He's keeping his cool, Sarah thought. *Even in the heat.* "Why?"

"I've done some things."

"No shit!" Gerard growled.

Sarah flashed him a glare, her emerging fury enough to get the deputy to shut the fuck up.

Kevin readjusted his glasses, undeterred. "Some things the Project wasn't too happy about," he said, his voice at an awkward disquiet. "I didn't do it the right way…their way."

As Sarah confronted him once more, Kevin gazed back down at his drink. His movements more rattled and restless. The mug now held in a trembling grip. *Confession time*, Sarah wondered…or hoped. "Did you kill someone who was innocent?" she asked.

No reply.

Sarah moved in closer, going in for the kill. "Someone who wasn't gonna be a murderer."

Keeping his eyes on the coffee's corpse, Kevin cracked up. "You're mighty suspicious, Detective."

"And why shouldn't I be!"

Letting the raindrops build up the tension, Kevin took his time. Not ready to answer yet.

Come on, fucker, Sarah's intuition complained. *Just give us the truth. Own up to it*! she wanted to scream. But instead, she stayed calm. Poised when one-on-one with what was rapidly becoming a psycho. "Who was it!"

Shaking his head, Kevin placed the coffee down. "It was the one they didn't want me to kill." Then, before a compelled Sarah could press further, the stranger faced her. "You've got a son, don't you, Detective?"

Sarah looked on, stunned. A chill overtaking her she couldn't contain. A fright not caused by the ensuing thunder, but one strong enough to shake off some of that sweat.

There was Kevin's smile still on display. Still taunting her.

How does he know that? Sarah wondered. She knew she was being obvious. Crumbling on what was supposed to be his interrogation. The confident detective's demeanor quickly fading fast to worried mother. *My Achilles' heel. He figured it out.*

Lunging forward, an irate Gerard pointed right at Kevin. A useless scare tactic. "We're talking about you, son! You understand?"

Recovering from the scare, Sarah pushed him back. "It's fine, Schaefer."

"We're talking about you and you only!" Gerard continued hurling at the suspect.

Sarah confronted Kevin's smirk. His calculating coolness back with a vengeance. *Time to go toe to toe*, she realized. "I have a son, yes," she said.

Gerard gave her a glare caught between concern and disapproval. One Sarah chose to ignore.

"How'd you know?" Sarah asked him.

Kevin tilted his head, playing off the instinctual intellect Sarah pegged him on long ago. "Just a guess." He grinned. "That's all, Detective."

Not buying it, Sarah chuckled. "Well, you sounded awful confident."

"I just think you're different, Detective." Kevin leaned back, the tight shirt on an even tighter chest making for a flirtatious flaunt. Kevin's gleaming smile and noticeable biceps showcasing some of the more appealing parts of his pretty boy package.

Not that Sarah could dare show appreciation. As much as it pained her. *He kills kids, dumbass,* she chastised her carnal desires. She glanced back at the journal in a frantic attempt at recovery. At restraining the thirst. "Well, why's that?" she struggled to get out. Not bothering to acknowledge Gerard's disapproving stare, she faced the sexy, if suspicious, stranger. "What makes me different?"

Kevin looked her up and down. An intense inspection, the grin not going anywhere. "You're *curious*, aren't you?"

Trying to save stoic face, Sarah just stared at him. No sifting or nerves flaring up. "Just answer the question," she said, her voice back to its detached distance.

Smirking, Kevin looked between her and Gerard's resting bitch glare, keeping the cops captive to his chilling confidence. His tempo. "Well, if we're laying our cards on the table." He fixated on Sarah. "I know quite a bit about you. Especially from the Retroactive."

Sarah matched his obsessive observation. Smoldering sparks may have very well shot off as the storm raged on behind them, but Sarah knew better. Especially when talking to a suspect. There was no smile or warmth on display. She was back to her scientific scowl. "Like what?"

Gerard stayed silent. He was too engrossed by this interrogation.

"I know you do well for yourself," Kevin said to Sarah. "Especially for this era." Like a clever scholar, he carried on with arrogance and smarts to spare. Nodded at the cell phone. "The 1970s aren't exactly a welcome time for a black female detective."

The truth pierced into Sarah's heart. But she sat still, showing no tells. No emotions...none outwardly at least. *He's not wrong. To be this crazy, the asshole is intelligent.*

"Especially in a town like this, Detective Barlow," Kevin went on. "I'd say that's pretty damn impressive." Then, with methodical slowness, he moved in closer, going one-on-one with Sarah. "And all by the age of thirty-one too."

Playing off this freakish conversation, Sarah waved at the Ziploc bag. "Did you get all that in your phone?"

Kevin's smirk remained.

"All my information's in there?" Sarah challenged.

"Everyone's is," Kevin replied.

An aggravated Gerard motioned at the cell. "So just call your little friends and have them pick your sorry ass up then!"

Kevin gave him a quick laugh. "I already told you. It's not that simple." He pushed his golden hair back. "My work here isn't finished, Deputy." He looked over at Sarah, basking in her intrigue. "Especially with you, Detective Barlow."

"So then tell us," Sarah said, keeping her tone steady and strong. "Tell us what you're here for." She pointed at the journal. "You already got Christine Falling—"

"Slaughter," Gerard interjected.

Disinterested, Kevin looked down at the phone.

Lost in thought or discomfort again, Sarah suspected. *Keep him on that spot, center stage when it's his turn to answer.* "So what else do you need from little ol' Perry, Florida?" she taunted the suspect.

A stifling moment lingered in the stifling heat. Sarah was ready to fire again-

"Tell me, Detective," Kevin started. He confronted her. "What exactly happened to Brandon's father?"

Gerard exploded. He stood up out of his seat next to Sarah, both his finger and cold glower aimed right at Kevin. "You shut the fuck up about her family!"

But Kevin was an apathetic statue. His gaze remaining glued to Sarah.

"You want me to cuff you and beat you right now!" Gerard yelled at the suspect. "It won't be the first time we roughed a son-of-a-bitch like you up!"

Kevin wants a reaction, that's all, Sarah reminded herself. But the more unsettling thought remained: *what if he does care*? As the adrenaline pulsed through her, Sarah clasped her hands together, anything to prevail in this psychological warfare. "That's a personal question," she said to the stranger.

Still scowling, Gerard sat back down. More upset there were no fireworks rather than getting to the heart of Kevin, Sarah figured.

"But it's nothing really," Sarah continued. Channeling her years of experience, she kept a stolid shield. Her most challenging effort yet. "We didn't get along... so he left." She shrugged. "We never got along anyway...and he didn't even want Brandon, so what was the point?"

Kevin nodded. "I see." A slight smirk appeared. "But you never think about him?"

"No," Sarah's sharp reply. "Never." *Which is true.* Sarah leaned back, keeping her eyes on the stranger. "He didn't wanna be around, and I'm doing just fine all by myself." She flashed an assertive smile. "I just didn't have time for playing housewife, I guess. All that American Dream shit."

Taking in her every word, Kevin gazed down at the journal. His collection, his "memories."

"I'm too busy being a detective," Sarah said. She paused. Not to hide the emotions but to embrace them. "Being a mom as well."

Kevin confronted Sarah. "But every boy needs a father."

At first, Sarah was surprised. But then the detective spirit took over. *Motive time,* Sarah wondered, her investigative intuition always attuned no matter the moment. No matter the scarce times she let her sentimental guard down. *Did daddy issues lead to killing kids?*

"That affects boys and girls, you know," Kevin said. "Abandonment from any parent. It can change their development."

Gerard's glare grew more intense, aimed right at Kevin the entire time.

"So, what are you trying to say?" Sarah asked Kevin. "Were your parents—"

With confidence to spare, Kevin shook his head. "I'm saying in general, Detective." He pushed his bangs to the side. "All these killers I have to execute. Most of them…they come from bad homes. Broken homes most of the time."

"I understand." But deep down, Sarah wondered where this was going. *What's his angle here?*

"So stay close to Brandon," Kevin went on. "Take care of him, love him. He needs that—"

"I do love him," Sarah said, unable to disguise her defensive side. Mama Barlow now overtaking the detective.

Kevin leaned in closer, his smile becoming cryptic. Staying on Sarah. "And I care about him too."

Thunder roared outside, the timing terrifying and dramatic.

The police department shook. Gerard jolted out of his seat. But Sarah and Kevin stayed put. Their showdown steady. The tape recorder capturing only silence rather than Sarah's racing thoughts…

Why's he saying this? she wondered amidst her more disturbing fears. *Who told him about Brandon? Why these concerns for me…for my son?* "Well," Sarah said, going toe to toe with Kevin's calm demeanor. She slid the journal in front of her. "I couldn't help but find the 2015 story interesting."

"*Story?*" Kevin scoffed.

Sarah smirked. "That year's a long way away."

"Not for me, it isn't."

Playing off his smug snark, Sarah opened the journal. "I just remember you talking about how personal that murder was for you."

Kevin grabbed the cup. "I'm not the murderer, Detective." He took an icy sip, never once looking away from the detective.

Keeping her detached persona intact, Sarah flipped to the 2015 account. "Right, sorry." She scanned the story. "But David Wash."

Kevin placed the mug down. "What about him?"

"I mean, it says here you grew up with him." Sarah pointed him to the page. "You went to school with him, correct?"

"I did."

"I don't know. It's just." Sarah stole a look over at Gerard. The deputy watching her like a supervisor. *He's still begging for confrontation.* "You really showed more passion here." She faced Kevin. "In the writing, you talked about redemption. How much you wanted to kill this guy."

Discomfort setting in, Kevin shifted in his seat. "David was a horrible guy. Always was."

"Right."

Desperate to stave off the self-reflection and anguish, Kevin readjusted his glasses.

Classic tic, Sarah thought. *He's nervous again…*

"I knew I had to get him," Kevin said, his voice losing the arrogant monotone. "I *wanted* to."

"So that was one of the few times you didn't feel any guilt?"

"Yeah."

"But what made it so personal?"

Kevin thought about it. His mask going from blank to melancholy. "I just. I always felt bad about what happened…what happened before I had the chance to go back."

"The girl," Sarah said. She glanced at the journal once more. "Michelle Beckley."

"Yeah. I wanted to really help her this time."

Sarah stared on at his remorseful eyes. The ones the glasses nor confidence could hide. "Yeah, it sounds like you did."

"None of them did shit," Kevin said. He waved at the journal, letting go of his pent-up regret. "They didn't do anything! They didn't wanna believe me!" He shook his head. "That he raped her, they just… Goddammit, they didn't do a goddamn thing!." Before the bitter breakdown could take over, Kevin took off the glasses and wiped his baby blues.

Putting a lockdown on the tears, thought Sarah.

"That's why I went out of turn," Kevin said. He jammed the glasses back on his face. "I don't care what they say. I had to!"

"What do you mean out of turn?" Sarah asked.

In professor mode, Kevin held his hands up, focusing on Sarah. "See at the Retroactive, there's a *certain* order you must follow."

"But why?"

"It's all about controlling outcomes! The butterfly effect. Everything must be a certain order to lessen the changes. The impact."

Sarah nodded, her fascination obvious. "Okay."

"Well, I." Kevin shrugged, offering no regrets. "I fucked up the order." He smirked out of weariness. Cynical disdain. "I couldn't wait. The memories and all…all the pain, I had to go ahead and take his sorry ass out."

Observing from afar (or as far as her curiosity would allow), Sarah watched Kevin's authentic pathos. Or at least what seemed authentic. *But what a fucking story…*

"That got me on the Retroactive's shitlist for sure," Kevin quipped. "And not the first time either."

Grinning, Sarah reflected on an answer. "That was the Edwards kid, right?"

"Yeah," Kevin chuckled. He slumped over the table, swept up in the recollections. "To them, I was just as dangerous. Just as evil." He faced Sarah. "Crazy, right?"

Sarah didn't reply. *Don't go too far with the crazy…*

"Hell, I think you're the crazy one, buddy!" Gerard barked.

Kevin sighed. "I don't know what I should've expected. No one wants to believe me. Never." He motioned toward Sarah. "I thought you'd be different, Detective! That you'd at least listen," he said, for once pleading.

Sarah hesitated. "I never said I didn't believe *some* of it."

Aggravated, Kevin turned away.

Until Sarah slid the journal a little closer. Grabbing Kevin's attention. His floundering hope.

"Let's see what else you got," Sarah challenged.

Kevin leaned in closer, eager. His smirk returning.

"Maybe you can convince us," Sarah went on. *Keep him talking.* She flicked through those final few pages, holding Kevin's gaze. "We've only got a couple more left."

Chapter 9

March 21, 1949

The ritual was routine but far from rudimentary. I still felt excitement. Dread. Adrenaline...all three at once. Even for kill number twenty.

Now I was on the hunt at night. Lorain, Ohio fucking freezing. A chilling forty or so degrees in what were empty city streets at the midnight hour.

My green sweater and black trousers fit well. The dark fedora a nice cover for my long hair.

I marched through the March coldness. No one around me on this sidewalk stage. The surrounding stores long closed. Not a car in sight. Even the streetlights looked asleep, not that their weak beams offered much support.

Folding my arms, I heard my footsteps form a repetitive rhythm. The only sound in this serene silence—

Until the sharp *SLAMS* sliced through this Tuesday night. A violent, aggressive attack.

Now the anticipation intensified, not to mention the subtle unease. Especially since I was about to come face-to-face with one of the most vicious serial killers in American history.

Breathing out cold air, I came to a quiet stop by a liquor store. Gathered my thoughts, all the courage I could muster. I knew

I was in the right place and time…but I wasn't sure I wanted to stay in the town a monster like Samuel Little grew up in.

I retrieved my phone. Pulled up the last text message the Retroactive sent: *30th Street. Tom's Goods.*

Ready for the job, I looked off toward a concrete street sign: *30th.* I was where they needed me, where The Choke And Stroke Killer was lurking as an eight-year-old boy.

Sure enough, I knew what the sounds were, who was damn sure making them, that is.

A *VIBRATION* pulled me from my pregame planning. I gazed down at my phone, at the Retroactive's latest text: *Samuel Little. Seven confirmed victims.*

As if I needed to be reminded of this asshole's atrocious rampage. But still, I'd see him (and kill him) as an African-American child. A product of Lorain's rampant racism and poverty. The kid didn't have much of a chance being born to a single mother. One who was in prison, and according to Little himself, a prostitute. Being raised by a single grandmother could only do so much. This guy was destined for hardship. For horror.

But still, I had a job to do. Samuel Little's reign of terror had to be stopped before it ever exploded into adulthood. Before he'd strangle so many innocents.

In that era, he could get away with killing prostitutes and people of color with no consequence. But not now. Not from justice served 2040 style.

The *SLAMMING* and *HARD HITS* continued. A soundtrack piercing through this weeknight's slumber.

Yet I stood there a few moments more. The big city blues still bothering me. I was alone in urban decay. All alone except for a few sleeping drunks I'd passed along the way.

I looked further down the road. Past a closed restaurant and bar, setting my sights on a small convenience store. The gas pumps extinct this late at night. The store's lights all out. But a hand-painted, hand-crafted swinging sign caught my eye: *Tom's Goods*.

My target was less than fifty feet away. An execution I needed not just for the Project but for those seven lives at stake.

Shivering, I adjusted my glasses. Took a deep breath. Some reassurance before I went in for the kill.

I advanced toward the spot, those *sounds*. Toward the stage set for Samuel Little and I.

There were alleyways along the way. Empty benches to match this town's desolation. But with every passing empty storefront, the louder the ruckus got. The attack not loud enough to awaken Lorain's many unsavory characters but brutal enough to pull me in closer.

Amidst the chills, I kept my sole focus on *Tom's*. As I reached the outskirts, there I saw a small shadow by the front door.

I stopped by the first pump. The rocking chairs remained still, every one of those windows nothing but pitch black. No lighting anywhere at all. The only thing I saw with life were the cobwebs.

And the young boy attempting to break into a Coca-Cola machine. Samuel Little as a child. He was focused. His crowbar crashing against the machine's metal.

Watching and waiting, I saw Samuel tear into the coin slot. Each successive swing further showcasing his developing strength. His face disguised by darkness. His animalistic grunts howling into the night.

The kid was tall and muscular for his age. Already showing the promise of being a professional boxer he'd later entertain but never fulfill. His poverty obvious. Patches covered his pants and beige denim jacket. Samuel wearing the shoes his grandma had probably given him several Christmases ago.

Holding my phone, I took a few soft steps toward that ferocious clanging. Closer to my target...

The familiar nerves returned. That anxiety before the attack. The Ohio breeze now further chilled me, further ravaged my soul.

Samuel's next guttural cry blared through the heart of the city. If Lorain had a heart, that is.

I stopped next to a garbage can, the boy within striking distance. Samuel too frustrated to notice me. Too focused on his "kill."

The steady hits sounded so vicious. Accompanied by Samuel's growls, what I was witnessing was a metallic massacre.

One that seemed beyond the brutal capabilities of a child. But The Choke And Stroke Killer was no ordinary child.

In my fascinated fear, I remembered how Samuel would become noted for his sketches. And here I was witnessing his artistry at work. The way he swung the crowbar, the brush to this battered Coca-Cola canvas. A similar sadistic skillset he'd employ for his seven victims.

The loudest bang then echoed. Like struck oil, coins poured from that busted slot. Finally, little Samuel could feast.

Moving quick, he pocketed all the nickels and dimes he could. Not worried about being discreet or checking his surroundings. His arrogant indifference making his five decades of death all the more improbable and impressive.

I took a deep breath. Trembling in the frigid terrain, I reached toward my belt. Toward the holster inside my waistband, where the Model 15 Smith & Wesson awaited this executioner's touch.

Samuel was still turned away. His funeral at *Tom's Goods* about to commence—

Suddenly, my phone *JOLTED* to life. The screen aglow with a new text from the Retroactive: *DO NOT KILL HIM!*

"What the hell…" I muttered.

Another *VIBRATION* brought another message: *90 VICTIMS CONFIRMED. DROP THE MISSION, KEVIN!*

"Hey!" I heard someone snarl. A deep, gruff voice ready to break free of adolescence. Of all sense of innocence.

I looked up to see who would become America's most prolific serial killer glaring right at me. The slaughtered soda machine standing behind him...his first victim. Gallons of pomade kept Samuel's hair swooped to the side, but the boy's face already hardened beyond his eight years. Those eyes without empathy. His crowbar ready to strike...Samuel Little ready to kill.

The nerves growing, I stared on at him. Paralyzed in the cold. In the fright.

Samuel's grip tightened on the weapon. I could tell he wasn't gonna back down. The monster didn't give a shit. When he wanted violence and torture, no one could stop him. Only me.

I knew what I had to do.

My phone buzzed again. Yet another Retroactive text, this one their most frantic yet. Their most demanding: *STOP, KEVIN! LITTLE AFFECTS TOO MUCH! STOP THE MISSION!*

Disgusted, I confronted Samuel. He was waiting for me to make the first move. The boy eager to start the killing spree twenty years early.

The iPhone kept convulsing in my hand. A cascade of incessant vibrations I chose to ignore. I knew the Project was calling. They wanted to let a psycho live because he killed *too* many people.

But this was yet another rule I wasn't gonna follow.

Beneath Samuel's glare, I retrieved the Smith & Wesson. In one hand, the phone shook with fury, the other latching on tight to the revolver.

Samuel didn't flinch when I aimed the gun at him. In the darkness, his young boxer body stood strong. The glower colder than these cold surroundings.

Feeling the phone pulsate over and over didn't stop me. The Retroactive was wrong. Saving ninety people can only *help* us. Especially when it came to extinguishing a monster that'd never change. Not when they were already pure evil.

I matched Samuel's anger. And damn sure didn't wait for him to attack.

Chapter 10

February 12, 1993

I couldn't stop. Even walking on this thin ice, the Retroactive couldn't keep me from doing what they needed me to do. What *I* had to do. I'd been on the prowl for several hours now, cold, hungry, bitter. The relationship between me and the job only getting more and more strained. More combative.

The Project no longer felt moral but instead manipulated. All those rules and for what? To protect innocent victims? What difference did it make that people witnessed me or that I refused to let the most prolific serial killer in American history live? If anything, I *saved* more lives. More than the Retroactive could ever imagine.

They knew they needed me. I was only given a warning for the fuck-up with Mack Ray Edwards's parents. And with the defiance I had with Samuel Little, all I got was a pay dock. Not many people could do this job, much less be as efficient as me. I suppose such a quality made me unique. You know...killing kids. One of the few traits I shared with some of my own disgusting targets. Who else could the Retroactive get for these assignments? Kevin was all they had.

But right now, Liverpool was cold, alright. Not quite snowing on this February afternoon, but such an ugly day didn't need any natural beauty. Not when I was about to come across a double dose of English Evil.

My long-sleeve red flannel shirt was no match for the biting wind. Neither was the skin-tight jeans. The breeze turning my hair into a fluttering blonde curtain. From Bootle's New Strand Shopping Centre to Liverpool's less cluttered city stress, I blended right into 1993's crowds and sights. No one paid me any attention. Not that there were many people out and about. Not the further and further I followed those two ten-year-olds through their journey to torture. Their victim a young boy: Tony Jones. And if I didn't stop his killers, Tony would never make it to his third birthday.

The more we approached desolation and this urban sea of abandoned businesses and soulless houses, the colder it got. The dread returned. The anticipation I couldn't help but feel…couldn't help but welcome.

I wasn't even British, but even I understood the horror…the morbid magnitude with which this crime played out. How not just England but the world struggled to wrap its head around two ten-year-olds in Robert Thompson and Jon Venables committing a murder most heinous.

What they were about to do to the young Jones child went beyond homicide and into torture, both psychological and mental. Even child molestation. There was no motive. No reason for why Tony Jones was chosen to die a most horrible death. But what lingered from this tragedy wasn't a mystery but the disturbing reality that the two murderers were children themselves.

When I was first dropped into Liverpool, I made the short trip to Bootle's mall. I watched those boys, Robert and Jon. Neither of them was tall orimposing. Their facial expressions veering between naive laughter and silent blanks. On the surface, they were normal enough…skinny, cute, hyper. Their energy obvious when they ran up and down the escalators and through the jam-packed stores. God knows, I struggled to keep up with them, and I'd been hunting down psychopaths for many months by then.

But besides youthful bliss, I caught a glimpse of the kids' darker side. Their shared sadism. They'd steal stuff and throw it down the escalators. Push other kids and adults out of the way like they were paparazzi getting in the way of their gleeful, cruel playtime.

Deep in my sickened soul, I recognized a few of those items Robert and Jon stole. The batteries they'd later jam in Tony Jones's mouth. The tube of blue paint they'd spray in his eye.

Keeping my distance, I watched them throughout the start of their sickening scheming. How they nearly took a young brother and sister at the TJ Hughes. How they *scouted* out other children at this 90s Paradise.

Of course, neither boy knew I was stalking the stalkers. I saw how they could've passed for literal blood brothers. Their dark hair and even darker personalities similar enough. Robert with a buzz cut and wider face, Jon with shaggy hair and angular features. Considering how close they were in age, they were on the same developmental path to demented maniac. Their young faces mirroring one another not in cute innocence but cruel indifference.

In my pocket, the phone kept buzzing. Text messages, phone calls, whatever complaints the Retroactive had I ignored. I was too focused. Too immersed in the hunt. I already knew what they'd say anyway: don't get too close to the targets, stay focused...all the rules giving them that fake sense of morality. Their authority.

But I behaved. I stayed in the shadows of strangers. Easy enough in a mall churning out clusters of customers while further propelling mass consumerism. Regardless of the Retroactive's bitching barrage, I never lost sight of those young killers. I was the best the Project had, of course.

Then finally, the boys found their perfect victim. There was no need to intervene when Jon first grabbed Tony Jones's hand. When right before all the indifferent cameras and witnesses, the two friends forced the two-year-old child out of the Shopping Centre. After all, I'd get to them soon enough.

As I followed the "lads" outside and into the brutal cold, I stole a glance at my phone. A quick glance considering the need to spay discreet, especially fifteen years before iPhones were commonplace.

But The Retroactive's text caught my eye: *Get to where you need to go! He's waiting!*

Smirking, I jammed the phone back in my jeans pocket. Readjusted my glasses against the wind, against the overcast sky. I saw those three kids walking fast down the sidewalk. Tony's hand pulled strictly by Jon's harsh strength. The little boy at their mercy.

Don't strike yet, I reminded myself. Wait 'til we get to the train tracks. Just two and a half miles away from Jones's grave.

There was still time before the murder. A good solid thirty minutes or so. But already, unease sunk itself into my skin. My shivers…and then came disgust.

Earlier I did my research. I knew all the close calls Jon and Robert had. The miracle it took for this tragic murder to even happen. How *no one* did anything when they saw Tony's tears or the piercing glares his killers had. The ferocious way with which way they'd lead the child to his death.

Trailing them, I saw the sad tragedy play out. The first stop an abandoned canal off the populated path. Lurking from afar, I saw the psychos push Tony to the scattered concrete, laughing as they made the boy hit his head several times. Laughing at the blood mixed in with his tears.

Wrath flowed into my veins. I wanted to pull out my 9MM pistol right then and there and gun these pieces of shit down like the rabid, disturbed dogs they were…But I had to wait. That painful, depressing wait. Forced to watch Jon and Robert continue assaulting the boy. Forced to watch Tony weep amidst the abuse as well.

My face got red. The anger warmed me in the cold, and into a rapturous rage I could barely contain. But one I had to. For now, at least.

An interruption cut through the eerie scene: my iPhone jolted to life. Immediately, I silenced the vibration but not before Jon Venables turned and looked toward the cluster of trees I hid within. Sure, there was no chance he saw me. No one usually did. But given the kid's sadistic glower, I would've never been able to tell anyway.

…Not until he gave Tony Jones another carefree kick in the ribs, that is. He and Robert's continual torture the signs I needed to know they hadn't seen me. Or that they didn't give a shit that someone was there to witness the attack. Their hysterical bloodlust too much to stifle.

I glanced down at my phone. At another one of the Retroactive's texts: *Get out of there, Kevin! Leave them alone and do your job!*

Per usual, I ignored their bitchiness. Their own twisted sense of ethics. I knew what I had to do. The Project's protocol didn't deserve to be followed to a tee.

Finally, Robert and Jon had enough of this pregame pain. Jon snatched Tony's hand yet again and led the crying child back toward the sidewalk. Back on that march to murder.

I lagged but stayed close enough for steady surveillance. Enough to trail those boys down the Liverpool streets. I knew what would happen next.

The trip was a struggle. Not so much from the way the killers treated Tony. They kept him close as he shed countless tears. Anytime he started to lag, one of the psychos would give him a quick kick to the ankle or a harsh shove. Anything to keep the poor kid going forward to his grave.

But what most unsettled me was Liverpool's indifference. The cold city streets offered cold reactions…or lack thereof. There was the elderly woman who told Jon and Robert to take Tony Jones to the police station. The various shopkeepers who questioned the two ten-year-olds. Even the murderers' friends who'd never seen the two boys with this mysterious small child they claimed was their younger brother. Tony still had the tears. The blood still trickling through his light brown hair and down his forehead. But no one went beyond a brief concern. No one phoned the police. No one stopped Jon and Robert from continuing on this dark descent. *No one did anything!*

Hell, I wanted to kill them on the spot. Even if the locals were "innocents" themselves. They couldn't be bothered to pull these three boys aside. To see past their forced facade of innocence. But instead, they let the psychopaths prevail. No one went the extra mile. No one took the extra time to see through the bullshit brother excuse. To see the *blood* flowing over young Tony's skin. To see his *fear*.

I had to restrain myself. My instinct to kill all things shitty. Instead, I let this scene continue to play out, this buildup to the brutal finale.

I followed the three of them toward the inevitable: the railroad tracks. The abandoned railway beyond the crowded strip. Far from any witness…except me.

Only a few shabby houses were nearby. A pitiful attempt at a neighborhood one step above public housing. The bland one-story brick houses and their narrow yards pitiful to more than just the naked eye. I didn't see much on this cold evening. Certainly none of the people who lived way the fuck out here.

By now, we were far removed from Liverpool's sidewalks and shops. I'd followed Jon and Robert out into the rural outskirts. A desolate forest on one side, abject poverty on the other. But the three kids were alone, and Robert and Jon were ready to "play."

And crouching by the outskirts of the woods, I watched. Gripped the pistol in my hand. The dim daylight doing nothing to disguise the ugly shacks. The swaying trees around me and the horror unfolding before me…

The two lonely railroad tracks were the stage. Those three boys the actors. I the captivated audience.

Like tombstones, pipes and iron bars were scattered near the tracks, amongst the dirt and stray grass. The railway rusty and rarely used. Except for now. For this execution.

Sweating instead of shivering, I clutched tighter to the 9MM. Felt my heart pound from a bombastic combination of anticipation and anxiety. Felt my soul twist with each punch or shove Robert and Jon gave Tony. Each cackle erupting from the killers' mouths. Each pathetic cry their victim struggled to release.

I now knew why Robert and Jon would go on to blame each other for the horrific crime. Both of them were the culprit. Feeding off of each other's developed demented bloodlust. Enjoying every second of the torment.

But still, I had to wait. Just a few more seconds, Kevin, I reminded myself. When they make their next move. Their final step from abuse to murder.

A sudden vibration startled me. Disrupted my reflection before the retribution. I snatched my phone and glared at the Retroactive's latest text:

Stop it, Kevin! Not them!

The next tremble didn't even make me flinch. Even when I was on the verge of another kill. At this point, I'd gotten used to the Project's bitchiness.

You know who to kill! Keep it clean! read their next message.

The loudest, most agonizing scream pulled my attention away.

Lowering the phone, I looked off toward the tracks. Now Tony was lying in the grass. Blood covered his skin and checkered sweater. The wounds worse. His voice too weak to scream again. The child too scared to crawl, much less fight back.

Robert and Jon stood over him. Their sadistic smirks more vicious than the blood-stained bricks each of them held.

Together, they scared the shit out of me. The sight of two ten-year-old psychos should've been surreal. Not possible. But the chills I got were all too real.

I knew what would happen next. I'd read about this terror too often. Prepared for this exact moment...this tragedy.

Toying with Tony, Robert pulled a tube of blue paint out of his pocket. One of the items he and Jon stole. The exact paint he was about to splash into Tony's eye.

It's time, I reminded myself. In the frigid wind, I straightened my glasses and stood up. Jammed the pulsating phone in my pocket, ignoring the Retroactive's persistent resistance.

Just as Robert started to lean in toward Tony, I charged straight toward the railway. Gun at the ready. My anger ablaze. No one would escape the death penalty on my watch. Not even children.

"Hey!" I yelled.

Frightened, both Jon and Robert jumped back, dropping their weapons. The tube hit the dirt, smearing blue into the blood.

Tony turned and looked at me. Through the tears, a faint glint appeared in his anguished soulful eyes. A rising hope...

I wasn't gonna let him down.

Robert waved his hands frantically, matching Jon's shivers pound for pound. "Please, we didn't mean to!" his whiny voice pleaded.

Glowering, I raised the 9MM. These hunters now the prey. The monsters no longer tough, now hiding behind the facade of youthful innocence. Their costumes. Those faint tears nothing more than makeup for their disgusting performance.

"Sir, please!" Robert said. "Don't—"

I fired a slug into his forehead. A perfect, unflinching shot. My aim always better when I had no remorse.

Stopping mid-speech, all Robert could do was turn toward his amoral accomplice. Robert's movements slurred, the bleeding bullet hole so small on the child's dying face.

Terrified, Jon couldn't even scream. Not that I'd give him time.

Before Robert collapsed, I gave the other killer an identical headshot. Right between the eyes. Clean kills much quicker than what the two assholes had in store for Tony...

Jon faced me. Stunned in his final fleeting moments. Blood dwindled down his face, matching the slow flutter of his closing eyes.

Robert hit the dirt first, then Jon. The murderers who killed together now buried together in adjoining graves. Their matching bulletholes the closest thing to a halo they'd ever get.

In the icy isolation, I lowered the smoking gun. There was no sadness. No inner turmoil. If anything, I felt fulfilled. And judging by Tony's calm silence, I imagined he felt relief.

I faced the boy and gave him a reassuring smile…the least I could do.

Still recovering from the fright, Tony just nodded. No longer crying, his face a portrait of confused innocence. His trauma inevitable but much more manageable than death.

The vibrating phone sliced through the serenity. Annoyed, I retrieved it. My glare fixated on the Retroactive's latest text:

We told you to leave them alone! They were not serial killers!

I scoffed in disgust. First, Samuel Little killed too many people, now Robert Thompson and Jon Venables had killed too *few*.

Another text hit me: *That's it, Kevin! We said Stephen Akinmurele! That's the reason you're there! You're done, Kevin!*

Their shrill phone call came next

Of course, I ignored it. Jammed the iPhone back in my pocket before looking over at Tony. The boy still kneeling there on the ground. Still silent. Still in childhood catatonia…not that I could blame him.

Clinging to the handgun, I turned my sights to those shacks. One of the most miserable houses was the childhood home of The Cul-De-Sac Killer. Stephen Akinmurele. The man I was sent to kill and only kill during my Liverpool layover. But I knew better. The

Retroactive was limiting itself, limiting the world. Why should a two-year-old like Tony Jones be left to die? This close to Akinmurele, the change of plans made too much sense. After all, why not kill two birds with one stone...or, in my case, three.

Those brick houses were still so hideous. A lower-class assembly line left to rot beyond the village. Essentially a continuation of the railway cemetery. Apparently, this whole area bred assholes.

And I didn't have to look too far for The Cul-De-Sac Killer. There was the skinny, tall teenager standing in an overgrown front yard. Or what this piss-poor community considered a front yard.

Like a slender scarecrow, Stephen Akinmurele stood completely still, glaring right at me. A wrinkled coat and jeans covering the Nigerian's light brown skin. His handsome features betrayed by a cold glower straight from Hell.

My chills returned once I realized he'd been watching us all along. The entire time. The torture, the massacre. The serial killer who'd go on to murder five elderly people had been an all too interested audience at fourteen years old. Then again, I guess I shouldn't have been too surprised, considering he had his first kill two years later.

In a sudden burst, Stephen turned and hauled ass inside. Straight into the shack.

I knew he was getting a weapon. His parents weren't home, not that they cared anyway.

Preparing for battle, I looked over at Tony. Our eyes locked for a brief second. Enough to convince me I'd done the right thing. His grateful expression said it all.

I could still feel my phone convulsing, but I didn't give a damn what the Retroactive had to say. Or if they were finally letting me go, or who knows, have me imprisoned. I had a job to do. Not for them but me. For the innocent people this sick asshole would go on to kill.

Raising the 9MM, I took off for Stephen's house. The first of many executions without the Project, I figured. At this point, I could go rogue. I had the phone, the notes, the names, so why the hell not? There's a lot of serial killers out there…

Chapter 11

Sarah slid the journal next to the tape recorder. Those stories stayed inscribed in her mind. She could even sense Gerard's unease, all while Kevin kept his lethargic coolness. His matter-of-fact mannerisms. The suspect nonchalant with his eerie entries.

"So, you did it anyway?" Sarah finally asked him, her drive for answers drowning out the nerves.

"I had to," Kevin responded. "Stephen Akinmurele had to die." He held up his hand, the fingers spread far apart for emphasis. "He killed *five* people, Sarah. Grandparents, for Christ's sake!"

At this point, the first name basis didn't bother Sarah. *He's just weird...too weird.* "So that's where your relationship with the Retroactive ended?" Ignoring Gerard's scowl, Sarah kept the spotlight solely on the stranger.

Kevin nodded. "Correct." Smirking, he leaned back in his seat. "In fact, they're coming after me now."

Some surprise struck Sarah. "After you?"

Forcing a sly smile, Kevin shrugged. "To them, I'm no different than what they're after." He leaned in closer, particularly zeroing in on the detective. "I'm a serial killer now, Sarah."

For a moment, Sarah wanted to correct him. Tell Kevin she wasn't convinced one way or the other. But she couldn't help but wonder if the combination of midnight and this hot-ass room was finally getting to her. *Stay focused*, she reminded herself. Sarah straightened her blouse. "So, are you just trapped here?" she said, struggling to keep her detached tone.

Gerard motioned toward Kevin. "Yeah, if you're such hot shit, why the hell did you kill that Slaughter girl?"

"He's got a point," Sarah said.

"Does he?" Kevin sneered.

"If the Project was helping you, how could you still have the ability to come to 1970 and kill Christine Slaughter?"

Kevin hesitated. The smug facade slowly giving way to uncertainty. Sarah and Gerard waiting with curiosity to spare.

Uncomfortable, Kevin had to readjust those glasses once more. "Look, there's a whole list of names." Struggling to shrug off the interrogation, Kevin looked over at the tape recorder. The bright red light beckoning his gaze. The mechanical stenographer capturing his every word. His every confession. "I know these killers. I studied them." He faced Sarah. "The Retroactive needs me a hell of a lot more than I need them."

"So what," Sarah said. "You're just deciding to become a vigilante on your own."

"I'm more than that, and you know it."

Sarah gave a weak chuckle. "Well, I don't know, man. You got us after you. Your own people don't even trust you—"

"But what I'm doing is right, Sarah." Kevin now honed in on the detective. "You don't realize how much you're gonna need me! You've got no idea."

"That's bullshit!" Gerard growled.

Matching Kevin's calmness, Sarah grabbed the bag. The iPhone. "But I don't understand." She couldn't help but notice Kevin's intense stare watching her pull out the phone. The device warm in her sweaty hand. Sarah surprised by its lightness. "How can you still travel if they're after you?" She held the phone up toward Kevin. "Is all the time travel just done through this?"

Kevin hesitated. Thunder blared outside, startling no one. The two cops hanging on to his answer. "Yes," Kevin said. "The phones, they're more than just communicating and research. We get updates on it. I can jump through time."

"That's one hell of a phone," Gerard scoffed.

Still so intrigued, Sarah glanced down at the device. "I see..." she said to Kevin.

Kevin smirked. "It is pretty important." He looked back and forth between Sarah and Gerard. "You *might* find out one day."

Thunder roared once more. But Sarah shook off the nerves. *Stay on him*, she reminded herself. *Stay on the phone.* "I'm just confused how it works." Playfully, she twiddled the phone side-to-side, showcasing its small, slender size. "How can something like this be so powerful?"

Kevin pointed at the iPhone. A confident challenge. "You sure you should've taken that out the bag, Detective?"

Nice try. "I think it's fine," Sarah grinned. *Two can play this game.* "I just wanna see how your world works."

"But wouldn't Sheriff Loomis disapprove?" Kevin said, keeping his voice at a dryness only belied by that steady smile. "I'm not so sure you two should be messing with evidence."

"She's got my approval," Gerard chimed in.

Kevin turned and faced the deputy's steely eyes.

"What? You hiding something," Gerard taunted.

"Not at all," Kevin replied.

"Well, how about you let us worry about the damn evidence then." Gerard's glower remained, the one sculpted exclusively for the suspect. "Just remember you're the killer, son. Not us."

Smirking, Kevin looked at Sarah, not even entertaining Gerard's masculine aggression. "I'm not the killer, Detective."

Moving on from the tension, Sarah placed the cell down. "Well, it is Labor Day, so I don't think anyone's gonna mind." She rested a hand on the screen, taking control of the conversation and Kevin's observant gaze. "But how can you stay going rogue like this? Won't the Retroactive track you down?"

Kevin shifted in his seat. A quick fidget.

Anything to not cave in. Sarah tapped the screen. "This is their equipment, after all, right?"

"I guess it won't be easy," Kevin responded, still staying so chill. "Because you're right. They're gonna come after me." Like a soldier resigned to his fate, Kevin leaned back. Channeling the cynical soldier he once was. "But it's worth it. They can keep chasing me, calling me a serial killer and trying to kill me, all that shit." He shook his head. "But I know what I'm doing's right... All those rules they got are just a game. Just an excuse to them. A way to look good in front of everybody else." He paused, savoring the spotlight. Savoring Sarah's attention. "But for me, I *care*! I give a damn! They've got no reason to play God and choose who lives and dies!"

Sarah leaned in closer. "But still, how are you gonna keep doing this." She pointed at the phone. "You said this runs on batteries or something like that."

"It does."

"So what happens when it runs out?"

Revealing that sly smile, Kevin sat up straight. "Well." In a methodical flourish, he readjusted his glasses. "Let's just say there are other ways to *travel*."

"But the Retroactive—"

"Look, they don't control everything," Kevin's sharp response. "I'll leave it at that."

Sarah could only chuckle. *Always got answers, always deflecting*. She scooped up the phone. "Okay, well, how do we turn this thing on?"

Kevin held his hand out. "Let me."

Gerard swatted his hand away. All brute strength and tenacious temper. "Just tell her, buddy!"

Annoyed, Sarah looked over at Gerard's red face. The heat and simmering hostility getting to him.

Laughing, Kevin held his arms up, playing along with Gerard's TCPD code. "Alright. It's cool, man."

Sarah faced him. "Well, what do I do?"

Taunting Gerard, Kevin looked over at him and pointed at the cell. "Can I at least show her, Deputy?" He stuck his hands up again. Twisting that snarky knife... "I won't touch anything. I promise."

Even Sarah smirked. Gerard fuming in a cold silence.

"Is there a button I have to press?" Sarah asked the suspect.

Kevin pointed her to the side of the phone. The small power button. "Just hold that down."

Sarah jammed her finger on it, eager to kick-start the strange device. Immediately, it cut on. Much to Sarah's surprise. Her amazement. *That 2040 technology must be ridiculous.*

"And that's all you gotta do," Kevin added.

Sarah's focus stayed on the screen. The current time reading: *12:16 A.M. Sunday, September 6.* There were layers of floating pictures. *YouTube, Yahoo!, CNN.*

"What the hell's all this..." Sarah said.

Smirking, Kevin ran his hands along his arms. "Those are called 'apps' where I come from." He gave Gerard's scowl a smile. "You know. 2040."

Sarah faced Kevin. "And this is where you get all this information?"

"Yeah. As a matter of fact, that's where *everyone* gets their information."

"Bullshit..." Gerard muttered.

Even more curiosity surged through Sarah, easing the humidity and tension. This was excitement. "I just, I don't know, Kevin." With a soft smile, she confronted him. "This is crazy."

"You still don't believe me?" Kevin teased. "Or should I say you still *don't want* to believe me?"

Control yourself, Detective, Sarah's skeptical side warned. *He's gonna be charming.* "Well, it's strange to think you'd go this far—"

"Shit, anyone could make this shit up!" Gerard interrupted. He gave the cell a dismissive wave. "Look at it. It's junk! Probably a prop from some stupid movie."

"Whatever helps you sleep at night, Deputy," Kevin remarked.

Before Gerard could go on the defense yet again, Sarah pointed Kevin toward the top right part of the screen. A yellow meter. *50%* "What does this mean? Is this the battery?"

Kevin smiled and nodded. "Yeah. That's how much it's got left."

"Only half?"

"Hey, that's plenty for me."

Unsettled by Kevin's indifferent attitude, Sarah looked on at the screen. "This is really all you need?"

"I can charge it depending on situation," Kevin said. He laid his arms on the table.

That figures, Sarah thought. *How convenient.*

"But what's Brandon doing right now, Detective?" Kevin asked.

What the fuck? Sarah immediately panicked. She faced Kevin's cool expression.

"I was just wondering where he's at," Kevin added.

Sarah hesitated. Struggling against an unease, not to mention her stoic professionalism…nevermind, Gerard's constant glances. "He's fine. Trust me on that."

"Is he?" Kevin challenged.

"Yes."

"Well, where does he stay?" Kevin clasped his hands together. "I'm just…curious."

Not giving in to Kevin's charming curiosity, Sarah brushed her bangs aside, deliberating on an answer. "His grandparents."

"Ah…" Kevin remarked.

"It's safe, you know," Sarah said, unable to hide a mother's defensiveness in her tone. "That's all I care about."

Kevin held his arms up, acting out a harmless aura. "I understand."

"It's none of your business anyway!" Gerard said in a Southern snarl.

"Oh, I know." Kevin looked right at Sarah, further adding to her anxiety. "I guess I just wanted to make sure the kid was okay."

"He is," Sarah replied.

Kevin stretched back, airing out his arrogance for the audience. "With you, I know."

What the fuck's that supposed to mean? Sarah wanted to ask. But she knew better. At least on the job. She needed to keep the focus on this time traveler, not herself. Especially not Brandon. *Stay on him, girl.* "What do you plan on doing now?" she asked, keeping her voice neutral.

"I've got some names. Especially some around here."

"Where? Florida?" Sarah responded.

Nodding, Kevin ran a hand through his hair. His headband as well. "Yeah. There's one, in particular, I'm looking into." He gave the cops a subtle smile. "One in Perry."

Sarah gave him a confused look. "You mean there's another killer?"

Gerard looked on at Kevin, keeping his pressure and anger at a hard tempo. "Didn't you just say Christine Slaughter was one?"

Thunder coordinated with Kevin's chuckle. "There's more than her, Deputy." His grin grew wider. "Way more than Christine Falling."

"You're full of shit," Gerard scoffed.

"There's plenty of serial killers, I'm afraid." Again, Kevin placed his hands on the table, latching into it, keeping those bright beaming eyes solely on Deputy Gerard John Schaefer. "Especially around here."

The discomfort obvious, Gerard shook his head dismissively. "Bullshit. You're fucking crazy."

From her perspective, Sarah saw Gerard tremble for once. Far from the tough guy he'd been playing all afternoon. The heroic hunk in shambles.

"This county's only got about thirteen thousand," Gerard went on, his anger the only thing keeping his voice sturdy. "So how many goddamn killers can be out here at once, huh?" He then leaned across the table, getting closer to Kevin's indifferent face. Flexing those impressive muscles for both the suspect and female detective. "Besides you."

In the Florida heat, Sarah looked over at the recorder. Their lone documentation for this wildness. *For such a story.* Her restless turmoil boiled. *I need more…the truth.*

Kevin offered a blank slate for Gerard. Nothing else. "I'm no killer, Deputy." He gave him a cold smile. "Not the serial killer in Perry, Florida at least."

"What the hell are you trying to say?" Gerard hurled at him.

"I think you know." Kevin's smile stayed put. Even when Gerard slammed his fist on the table.

"You son-of-a-bitch!" Gerard cried.

Kevin's cryptic cackling startled both Gerard and Sarah.

"Just confess, asshole! Tell us the truth!" Gerard yelled.

"I told you everything," replied Kevin's typewriter tone. Never once did he shy away from Gerard's focus. Or Sarah's. "I'm sorry it's not what you wanna hear, Deputy."

Lunging forward, Gerard snatched Kevin's velour shirt collar. Ready to strike fear in the stranger, even if Kevin remained unresponsive. Remained cool. "Yeah, what would your ass say in jail, huh? When I get you in that cell!"

"Gerard, stop!" Sarah pleaded.

Both Gerard and Kevin looked toward her as she held the phone out.

"Here, just show us," Sarah told Kevin.

Gerard glared at her. "Sarah—"

"Let's just see what it does!" Sarah said. She faced Kevin's intrigued expression. "If you can prove anything." She jammed the phone into Kevin's weak grip, the stranger surprised by her sheer determination. The cop's curiosity. "Show us who your next target is. The one in Perry."

Still unconvinced, Gerard motioned toward Sarah. His controlling demeanor taking over. "Are you sure about this, Sarah—"

"Detective," Sarah corrected. "And absolutely."

Kevin pulled the phone in closer, indulging in its offerings.

Anxious, Gerard watched the stranger's every move. Particularly how fast they typed on that phone. How fast Kevin scanned it.

Sarah grabbed Gerard's arm, pulling him in closer toward her. "Let's just see what he comes up with," she whispered.

"But what if he's crazy!?" Gerard replied, unable to keep his voice low.

Kevin grinned at them. As handsome and poised as ever. "For starters, how about Christine Falling?" He showed them the screen.

There was the round face. An adult Christine's dull, monotone expression in that mugshot.

Engrossed, Sarah grabbed the phone. A closer look at the article. Indeed, Ben and Patsey Slaughter were Falling's parents. Her sister Tina. Her birthplace Perry, Florida. The murders all documented around the early eighties.

Sarah went into a restless silence. Especially when she saw the sources included on this.... *com* page. *The New York Times, The Tallahassee Democrat, The Atlanta Journal-Constitution*...even Perry's local paper: The *Perry News-Herald*. Sarah stared on, hypnotized by the image of their little dead victim, all grown up to be a child killer. *Whatever this is, it's pretty goddamn convincing*, she thought.

"Fucking bullshit!" Gerard grumbled, unable to disguise the rising concern. "He's full of shit, Detective!"

But the cryptic allure pulled Sarah right in. She handed Kevin the phone back. "Who else?"

Kevin now showed the smirk. The confidence. "Do you really wanna know?"

Immediately, Gerard sat down. His face full of fear rather than ferocity. The cracks beneath the strong surface starting to show...

Sarah sat back in her seat. "Yeah, tell us."

Kevin's gaze locked in on Gerard's glower. "I'll show you."

Sarah waved toward the iPhone as Kevin typed some more. "All that's on there?"

"Yeah," Kevin said. He held the screen in front of them. Kevin keeping those piercing bright eyes on Gerard...blades behind glasses.

Gerard returned no emotion. Certainly nothing human.

"Here he is," Kevin said.

The video was easy to see in 2040 HD. Crystal clear footage.

"This is who I *really* came for," Kevin added.

What the cops got was a montage. Quick cuts of security video leading from Sally's Diner in Fort Lauderdale, Florida to an unknown mobile home in Perry. A mobile home of horror.

But the cell phone wasn't playing a movie with a happy ending. What Kevin held was recorded snuff.

The living room was straight out of the era. A bulky T.V., leather sofa, and shag carpet. The lighting vivid and bright. The record player working overtime on The Beatles' "Something."

There was screaming and a struggle. The only thing more striking than the television's rabbit ears Deputy Gerard John Schaefer's Smith & Wesson.

A slightly younger Gerard held the skinny young woman in his arms. Her hands tied behind her back, a rag stuffed in her mouth. Still in uniform, the deputy taunted and teased her, maneuvering that revolver up and down her body. Making her cringe when he ran the barrel through her long, curly hair...The twenty-two-year-old woman having no chance of escape. Gerard would make damn sure of that.

The audio was low, but enough eeriness could be heard, particularly how loud Debra Thomas squirmed in Gerard's arms. A creepy contrast to the sadistic softness of the deputy singing along to the Fab Four.

In the interrogation room, Gerard stood up, disgusted! The storm unable to match his outrage. "What the hell is this?" he shouted.

Kevin kept his chilling stare on him. "I came for you, Deputy." His hand held the phone tighter. Tighter to that video. "This is where I get *all* my evidence."

Shocked, Sarah kept watching them. Caught in the crosshairs of this showdown. Too curious to intervene. Too curious to not see where Kevin and his phone led them. Especially when the video showed more violence. Showed Schaefer throwing the diner waitress to the ground.

"You're fucking crazy!" Gerard yelled at Kevin. "That's not me!"

Not breaking eye contact, Kevin held the phone closer to the two cops. "That's you, Deputy! You kidnapped her after work before killing her!"

Sarah noticed the sweat streaming down Kevin's hairband. Not to mention his rare emotion. His unrest regarding the footage. The murder.

Gerard trembled in the heat.

"You killed her!" Kevin hurled at him.

"No!" Gerard yelled. "I didn't!"

Holding the iPhone, Kevin looked over at Sarah, holding her gaze. "This is what he becomes, Detective! This is why I'm here!"

Full of rage, Gerard slammed the table, letting the tape recorder go airborne for a second. "Goddammit, I didn't kill anyone!"

Kevin stood up, making sure to put that screen even closer toward Gerard's glower. "You murdered her! You know you did! You got her jewelry at your house right now!"

Gerard turned away, somewhere between upset and unsettled...

"They'll find it!" Kevin added. "Debra Thomas's gold tooth too!"

Now it was Sarah's turn to stand. Keeping her cool, she staggered up from her seat. Her sharp mind more disgusted once she saw Gerard ready to strike Debra in that video. "You mean this is in the future?" she yelled at Kevin.

"It's not the future," Kevin immediately replied. "It's the past!"

Gerard glared at him. "You son-of-a-bitch!"

Panicking, Sarah struggled to lean in between them. She pointed at the video. The homemade snuff. "This is real!?"

"Yes!" Kevin replied.

Upon Kevin's reveal, Gerard retrieved his pistol.

"He's a serial killer!" Kevin told Sarah. For emphasis, he held the phone up to Sarah specifically. Just in time for her to see Gerard onscreen slapping Debra!

"I didn't do nothing!" Gerard yelled. "That's not me!"

Besides the storm, Debra's helpless screams formed the soundtrack. Surrounding the small room. Straight into Sarah's mind.

Behind compelled eyes, Sarah watched the deputy point the gun at Debra. His handsome face a vicious shade of red. The evil excitement well on display. A release of his deepest, darkest desires. *He's enjoying every second*, Sarah thought amidst the whirlwind of violence both on-screen and off. Sarah's fear now joined by propulsive adrenaline. *It's him! How did Kevin get this!?*

"It's not me, I swear!" Gerard struggled to yell. His sobs crushed the cop's grit. "I didn't mean to! I swear..."

Playing projectionist, Kevin kept holding the phone for Sarah. Unfazed by Gerard's trembling grip on the gun. The deputy's outburst hitting histrionics.

"There was voices!" Gerard yelled at them. "They wouldn't stop! She wouldn't fucking stop!"

Then Sarah watched the inevitable horror: Gerard's wild grin on screen. The first shot to the head forever silencing Debra's scream. Then the second sending blood over his smile. Over that badge.

Full of disgust, Sarah turned and glared at Gerard. By now, he was a whimpering mess. A psychopath reduced to tears. Shivering in the stifling spotlight. *He's sick. Kevin's right. He's been right all along.*

"You killed her, didn't you!" Sarah accused Gerard. She motioned toward the phone. "When'd you do this, Gerard!"

Hanging on to that Smith & Wesson, Gerard stumbled on his words. On all emotions except panic.

"December eighteen, 1969," Kevin answered, his voice full of that calm confidence.

"You did it," Sarah scolded Gerard. "Goddammit, you killed her!"

Kevin lowered the phone, his slow movements so smooth. "There's more."

Gerard faced him. The tears and sweat unable to hide that chilling glower. The killer's wrath.

"There's Ann Walker," Kevin said.

Crumbling under the confrontation, Gerard shook his head. "No! You lying son-of-a-bitch!"

"Then there's all the other girls he's gonna keep killing," Kevin went on, staring the deputy down like a heartless judge. "The ones who'll keep dying and keep going missing. All because of him."

Caught up in her own captivated curiosity, Sarah looked back and forth between the two men. *Let Kevin keep going*, she told herself. *He's pushing him.*

"All the way up 'til his sorry ass gets arrested in 1973," Kevin said.

With an anguished roar, Gerard put the gun to Kevin's face. "I can stop! I've stopped killing before, Goddammit!"

Sarah's scowl fixated on Gerard. No longer enjoying the hunk but horrified by him. By his obvious malevolence.

Playing off Gerard's rage, Kevin stayed at his own lethargic pace. "For now. But it'll come back. It always does."

"No…" Gerard struggled.

"That pain, Mommy and Daddy's disappointment." Kevin's smug smile returned. "They're gonna be even more disappointed when they find out that not only is their son a complete fuckup, but also a perverted rapist and serial killer."

Weeping, Gerard waved the gun at him. "Fuck you…" he whimpered. "You son-of-a-bitch…"

Sarah kept her distance. Too immersed to intervene at this point. *He's getting to him.*

"That you're a crossdresser. You wear panties," Kevin kept chiding Gerard. "That you've had sexual fantasies since you were a kid, Gerard! Violent fantasies!"

The tears matched those raindrops. Gerard closed his eyes. Remorse only for himself. The past.

"Bondage, killing animals," Kevin went on, his tone steady and sharp. "You're one of the reasons why I gave up on the Retroactive! I should've been assigned to kill you when you were a little sick fucking boy, Gerard. Not after you've already murdered two young women, you sick fuck!"

Gerard now glared at him. Gone were the tears and vulnerability. He was back to being the scary serial killer.

Shit! Sarah thought.

Not relenting, Kevin ended the video. With one tap, he brought up a new page. A new picture for his audience: a black-and-white mugshot. There was Gerard smiling, his hair combed, his shirt pressed, his dimples on point. All those years of killing hadn't taken a toll on his good looks and muscles.

"There you go, Gerard!" Kevin yelled. "This is what happens!"

Everything about the photo was authentic. All too familiar from Sarah's perspective. The letter board, the stark style, the height chart. *How could he fake this? That's Gerard!*

And the year further unsettled her: 1973…Sarah's intuition and suspicion all came to the same conclusion: *He's telling the truth! He's here for a reason.*

Out of the corner of her eye, Sarah saw Gerard lean in closer, going in for the kill. He was a rabid dog of a deputy. One armed with a pistol rather than teeth.

But Kevin didn't care. He held the mugshot up higher, matching Gerard's every move. "You get arrested in 1973, but I'm here to end your sorry ass now!"

Snarling, Gerard knocked the phone out of Kevin's hand.

Kevin now rushed toward the other side of the table. Sarah's side. His steps fast and furious.

Sarah reached toward Kevin. The panic putting her in a fearful frenzy. *Help him.*

Only she found out fast Kevin didn't need any help.

Kevin snatched Gerard's wrist with an assassin's efficient quickness, keeping the pistol down and at bay. His left hand went toward Sarah's waist. Right to her holster.

Sarah didn't have time to react. No one did. Not even the certified serial killer she'd spent the last year working with.

Struggling to break free, Gerard's glare grew more enraged. Frustration mounting at meeting someone who could fight back. "Let go of me, Goddammit!" he roared.

Kevin retrieved the Smith & Wesson and pointed it at the deputy's face. Inches away from that fiery scowl. That bitter expression all too common for executions…

Gerard was left at nothing to look at Kevin's persistent grin.

Sarah just watched. Stunned and entranced. Knowing there was no need to step in. How could she when this was justice served from the all-too-distant future? *He saw my holster all along! He planned this! Everything…*

Caught in the calm crosshairs, Gerard kept squirming. "You fucking faggot!" He drew his other hand back, desperate to escape through one brute punch. "Let go of me!"

But the smile didn't fade. Not even as Kevin pulled the trigger and sent blood and brain bits all over the interrogation room's dismal decor.

First, Gerard's gun *SMASHED* to the ground. Then came the heavier tumble. Literal dead weight.

A crimson curtain coated the one-way mirror, making Kevin's flared pants even redder.

Sarah wiped the death debris off her face. Getting a clearer view of the fatal gunshot. The blood now more prevalent than the sweat stuck to her skin…

Kevin, too, looked like he'd emerged from a red rainstorm. But he was still chill, unfazed, he used his shirt as windshield wipers for those glasses.

The smoking barrel couldn't hide Gerard's corpse sprawled out on the stained floor tile. Part of his face excavated by one brutal bullet. The flesh mushy with tattered pieces sticking straight up.

"Jesus Christ…" Sarah muttered.

She couldn't turn away. Only one of Gerard's baby blues remained, a striking marble amidst the mutilation. Blood kept streaming from this human volcano, pouring past the spiked skin and down Gerard's neck. All the way down to a tarnished badge.

Raindrops got louder in the eerie silence. Slowly snapping out of her unnerved shock, Sarah looked over at Kevin.

He stuck the glasses back on. The remaining red dots and minor brain particles not too much of a hindrance. Kevin flashed that smile at her. "Don't touch this." He placed her gun on the table. "It's got my fingerprints on it. They won't blame you."

A million questions, a million hypotheticals marched through Sarah's mind. But she didn't know where to start. Still too stunned from the sudden gunshot. The sinister secrets. This mysterious stranger.

"They'll just blame me," Kevin reassured. "They don't have the resources or information on serial killers anyway. Not yet."

"What..." Sarah mumbled.

Kevin grabbed Sarah by the shoulders, staring into her soul. "Look, I'm the killer, alright! That's all you gotta tell them, Sarah."

Take control, Detective Barlow. Sarah took a step back, breaking away from Kevin. Breaking away from the nerves and confusion. "So you're just gonna leave?"

"I've got no choice." He rushed toward his phone. For once, a panic showing through the easygoing armor. No longer was Kevin smiling.

"But still!" Sarah said, unable to contain her inquisitive intuition. The need to know. "Why here? Why'd you come here for all this?"

Ferocious thunder made the lights flicker. But that didn't slow Kevin's movement. Nor Sarah's personal investigation.

"You came here just for Gerard?" she said as she stopped near him.

Kevin grabbed the iPhone. "I already told you." He confronted Sarah. "There was Christine Falling and Gerard Schaefer. I could take them both out. Two birds with one stone, remember."

With impulsive speed, Sarah snatched his arm. Her strength surprising Kevin. "But why leave? You can stay, we can learn more about you—"

Showing simultaneous respect and restraint, Kevin held her back. "I can't. They're gonna come after me, and I can't. I can't risk that!"

Sarah relented, giving in to a defeated silence. *This is beyond you, Sarah. Beyond 1970.*

Kevin sighed. Reluctant to show regret. The rawest of feelings the most unfamiliar for him: vulnerability. "Look, maybe I'll come back one day, but I have to keep moving. To them, I'm...I'm a killer now. I'm no different than what we hunt!" Like a flustered professor, he took off his glasses. "I'm the last serial killer."

Barely staving off the breakdown, Sarah turned away. "But I don't understand—"

"I've got no choice, Sarah! To get rid of all these assholes, I gotta break the rules. I'll be the killer in the history books, but I don't fucking care!" He put the glasses back on. "I'll make the world *perfect.*"

Sarah took another step closer and motioned toward the phone. Toughness the only thing holding back tears. "But how? The phone's about to die."

Kevin tapped his glasses' skinny temple. At his touch, a faint red light tinted the lens. A secret component. "I got other ways."

Sarah had to chuckle. *It's just getting weirder and weirder.*
He could've left all along. This was always part of his plan. "I
should've known."

"The glasses are faster for travel." Kevin gave her an
awkward grin. "But hey, there's another reason I came here."

Held captive to his words, Sarah looked on at him. *Fuck it. I
need to know.* "What."

Kevin stepped back toward the table, toward the tape
recorder. "It's about you." He slipped the phone into his pocket.
"And Brandon."

Now Sarah let her obsessive side take over. She snatched
Kevin's arm once more. Feeling an adrenaline in the bicep, an
unease Kevin couldn't hide now. "What is it?"

Struggling with his emotions, Kevin hesitated. His face back
at a blank. He avoided all eye contact. Avoided the concern of both
a loving mother and devoted detective.

Sarah shook his arm. "Kevin, tell me!"

"It's... it's nothing." Kevin forced a smile. "Just take care of
him, will you?"

The sincerity soothed Sarah. She began to loosen her grip.
Brandon's home, he's safe, she reassured herself.

"He'll be okay as long as you're around," Kevin went on.

Giving herself space, Sarah staggered further back. She
looked on at Kevin, not ready to reply yet. Her mind too consumed
by memories. By Brandon.

"I made sure of that, Sarah," Kevin added.

The dread still within, Sarah pushed her bangs aside. "What do you mean?"

"Samuel Little was gonna kill you."

That dread turned into outright fear. "No…What…"

"He was gonna murder you in 1972," continued Kevin's robotic tone. "When you were in Ocala visiting your sister."

Tears formed in Sarah's eyes. Because deep down, she knew Kevin hadn't been wrong yet. *He knows about Marla.* "You saved me," she mustered out.

"I did," Kevin said. He surveyed the room, the carnage. "I also stopped another killer."

This next revelation made Sarah's heart pound. Created more sweat. More fright. The most anxiety the detective had ever shown. "Who?"

Kevin confronted her. His expression as close to empathetic as possible. Only he was in no rush to answer…

Aggravated and rattled, Sarah slammed her fist on the table. "Who? Tell me!"

Loud footsteps erupted from outside. Frantic footsteps running right toward the interrogation room.

Startled, Sarah faced the door as it burst open.

There entered the rook, a young pale deputy Sarah had seen around but damn sure didn't know by name. His chubby frame staggered inside. His shivers giving way to a shrill shriek once he laid eyes on Gerard's dead body.

But Sarah had someone else on her mind. She turned toward the table. The *empty* room. Gone was the tape recorder, the journal. Gone was Kevin.

All the anticipation died on the spot. The wondrous possibilities. Instead, an emptiness replaced Sarah's excitement. A void in her heart. *Where the hell is he?*

In the height of the deputy's alarmed screams and the storm's frightening thunder, Sarah rushed up to the table. Splashing through red puddles in this literal race against time.

She came to a weary stop. The stage abandoned save for this bloodbath. *He's gone!* Such finality didn't so much scare as sadden her. *He won't come back, Sarah! Not ever in your lifetime.* Disappointed, Sarah glanced down at the table. The spot where she conversed with the stranger well into the night.

And the spot where a thick file now awaited her. A dark blue one. And one that hadn't been there before.

"He got away!" she heard that deputy scream in the hallway. "He killed Gerard!"

Just like how Kevin told her they'd know he did it, Sarah thought. She picked up the folder. Its material much sturdier than the Manila bullshit they were stuck with.

Sarah didn't recognize the logo. The illustrated bulging eyeball etched on the surface. Nor did she recognize the department name: *United States Serial Killer Studies*.

"What the fuck...?" Sarah said.

Her eager intrigue came back with a vengeance. Sarah opened the file.

All around her, she heard more footsteps. More screams. More of the storm's scary music.

But nothing struck Sarah more than the images and articles in her hands. The file on Brandon Barlow.

The only photos she recognized were ones from his childhood. The ones she took of her son in the years before he became known as The Inheritor. A man who killed over twenty women up until his arrest in 2025...when Brandon was sixty years old.

Various notes and newspaper articles further highlighted the way Sarah's son would hack up his female victims. Most of them prostitutes, some he met online, even a pre-teen. His sickness didn't stop. Nor did his slaughter.

But the motive was obvious to the Studies' experts. And the motive was what ultimately gave Brandon his chilling moniker. How he must've "inherited" the evil from whoever strangled his mother, Detective Sarah Barlow, all those years ago. A murderer that turned out to be the prolific Samuel Little.

One of the last pages showed the Studies' final ruling: *The Retroactive Project*. Brandon's executioner only had his first name listed. But Sarah didn't have any doubts who it was. She now knew the identity of the other killer Kevin had been assigned to. The one Kevin ultimately abandoned.

Sarah let the tears go. Tears of joy, tears of horror. She had to believe the case file at this point. Kevin put it here for a reason.

All the articles shook her to the core. The photos of a man that grew up to no longer resemble the cute child she raised but instead to become an American monster.

Even the photos taken in his teen years and early twenties never showed Brandon's smile. The introspection was still there. The good looks. The tall, muscular frame that would later help him kidnap innocent victims. But there was a hardened coldness in those constant glares. A hate eager to escape. The culmination of growing up in the shadow of a murdered mom…or at least, that's what Sarah hoped was the cryptic catalyst.

Goddammit, Brandon! she sobbed both inside and out. Her soul slowly squeezed by the sorrow. *Not you, baby. That's not you…*

Finally, Sarah went to the very back of the folder. Unable to look at the grisly details and crime scene photos. Those pictures of her son The Inheritor.

But there was one Polaroid left. One that Sarah hadn't seen in years. Brandon at three years old. Playing with a Scooby-Doo doll in their old apartment. He wasn't smiling here either, but his comfort was obvious. His joy.

"Just take care of him, will you?" Sarah remembered Kevin saying.

She reached out and caressed her son's face. Just like she would when she got to her mom's house Monday morning. What she'd now be doing well past 1972…

"He'll be okay as long as you're around," Kevin had said.

A smile crept across Sarah's face. Her sobs weakened. The melancholia reassured by a scribbled message at the bottom of the picture. The handwriting all too familiar: *It's not too late.*

In her relieved mind, she could hear Kevin's calm voice once more: "I made sure of that, Sarah."

THE END

Author's Note

Where to begin. Well, a while back, I told myself I wasn't gonna write a novel based on an old screenplay. That was my goal, my challenge. The only problem was I wrote something in between. Maybe more novella than novel, but hey, *The Last Serial Killer* can be considered an anthology of sorts, so cut me some slack.

Anyway, I decided to base this one on two of my more popular NoSleeps. And those of you who've been following me awhile probably recognized both the John Wayne Gacy and Mary Bell stories from my old subReddit. I always considered Kevin's trials and tribulations a half-ass series I never got around to finishing, so here it finally is for those who care! Who knows? Maybe there's room for a sequel.

I think the concept itself is rich and interesting. Maybe the most high-concept thing I've ever done. I also enjoyed branching out more into the sci-fi and action genres while obviously still keeping this bad boy firmly rooted in my horror/thriller wheelhouse.

Maybe on a subconscious level, what made these initial stories so popular was the wish fulfillment of revenge so many people have. I guess that can be tied to Tarantino's great recent movies like *Once Upon A Time In Hollywood* and *Inglourious Basterds*... however, the ironic thing is I actually don't believe in capital punishment.

So this was a fun one to write. For those curious, I did my research for each era's fashion, mood, and, yes, pistols of choice. I gotta say, I enjoyed it. I love history, particularly pop culture history. And as someone who loves The Golden Age Of Hollywood and 1960s rock, I had a blast pre-planning. The only real concern I had was debating whether to include the names of real victims and family. I opted not to out of respect for those real-life victims who endured horrors well beyond my dark imagination.

On a lighter note, the final twist involving Brandon didn't come until I got closer to writing chapter eleven. Yeah, I usually outline like hell, so most of this plot was already laid out, including the confrontation with Gerard. But Brandon's twist (and the glasses) didn't quite hit me until I was prepping the last chapter. Initially, there'd be the shock that Kevin "saved" Sarah from Samuel Little, but then I got to thinking, "Damn, he needs more motivation. He's traveling from the future and barely knows the good detective!"

As for where the initial inspiration for this story came from, I guess it's how much we all find fascination in the disgusting serial killers walking among us. I'm not ashamed to admit I do as well. But around December was when I wrote the Gacy story, and needless to say, I already had enough decent information on him to accurately capture his childhood. I always enjoy writing about the past, so around then, I was excited to write about the early fifties, especially about a different state other than my beloved

Florida/Georgia neck of the woods (another cool thing about the novel was getting to cover so many different locations and eras).

But I can't say for sure where this killing serial killers as kids concept came from. Somewhere deep in my crazy mind, I suppose. But I do have one theory: my horrific experiences spent teaching seventh grade English at a title 1 public middle school. Hey, I lasted ten weeks! As wild as the kids were, I enjoyed them, but yeah, administration, politics, and parents were all goddamn terrible. Complete assholes. I suppose such a miserable experience contributed to me developing that Gacy story. Not to mention my own curiosity about reading how future psychopaths were as children…their warning signs, that eternal debate of nature vs. nurture. All interesting stuff, really.

I hope y'all enjoyed the read! Thanks for checking it out! Thank you Ashley, Holly, and the folks for always supporting me. Thank you Ash and I's lovely cat Patches for *emotionally* supporting me. Big shoutouts to my OG fans like Sharlene, Marc, Sherrie, and Skyler! Stay safe, everyone! Y'all know how prolific I am, so stay tuned.

Rhonnie Fordham

August 12, 2020

Printed in Great Britain
by Amazon